# God Bless You, Otis Spunkmeyer

Also by Joseph Earl Thomas

*Sink*

# God Bless You, Otis Spunkmeyer

## Joseph Earl Thomas

GRAND
CENTRAL

New York Boston

Grand Central Publishing
Hachette Book Group
1290 Avenue of the Americas, New York, NY 10104
grandcentralpublishing.com
@grandcentralpub

First Edition: June 2024

Grand Central Publishing is a division of Hachette Book Group, Inc. The Grand Central Publishing name and logo is a registered trademark of Hachette Book Group, Inc.

The publisher is not responsible for websites (or their content) that are not owned by the publisher.

The Hachette Speakers Bureau provides a wide range of authors for speaking events. To find out more, go to hachettespeakersbureau.com or email HachetteSpeakers@hbgusa.com.

Grand Central Publishing books may be purchased in bulk for business, educational, or promotional use. For information, please contact your local bookseller or the Hachette Book Group Special Markets Department at special.markets@hbgusa.com.

Library of Congress Cataloging-in-Publication Data
Names: Thomas, Joseph Earl, author.
Title: God bless you, Otis Spunkmeyer / Joseph Earl Thomas.
Description: First edition. I New York : Grand Central Publishing, 2024.
Identifiers: LCCN 2023054988 I ISBN 9781538740989 (hardcover) I ISBN 9781538741009 (ebook)
Subjects: LCGFT: Novels.
Classification: LCC PS3620.H6285 G63 2024 I DDC 813/.6—dc23/eng/20231204
LC record available at https://lccn.loc.gov/2023054988

ISBNs: 9781538740989 (hardcover), 9781538741009 (ebook)

Printed in the United States of America

LSC-C

Printing 1, 2024

By choosing and extolling certain models
to the exclusion of all others, he sought
to deny the impending crisis of his own
self-representation.

—John Keene, *Annotations*


So you say you're under a curse? Well, so
what? So's the whole damn world.

—Jigo to Prince Ashitaka, *Princess Mononoke*

# God Bless You, Otis Spunkmeyer

OF ALL THE LEVEL 1 trauma centers in one young though very old nation, it's this one, on the north side of a northeastern middling city where we wear teal scrubs stained with shit which, in this context, helps signify the unbearability of true pleasure in the world. Pleasures in feeling purposeful and needed and useful without forcing the disambiguation. The waiting room is full. In the trauma bay, bright lights illuminate the bleached-out bloodstains and pennies thrown across the tile floor; a small boy is shot through the thigh again with an AK-47, and next door a teenage girl from Temple is sexually assaulted. This homeless dude Greg who everybody loves to lovehate is beaten to near death outside a gas station by teenagers who are not yet shot through their daddy's deep blue Crown Vics with AK-47s at Sunoco on Broad and Lehigh or Hess on Chelten Ave, or Exxon by the Home Depot where I once

worked in the Lawn and Garden section and Hector
and them waited outside by the truck for gigs playin ball
with every single mom's little kids on that Fisher Price
court in front of where Lorenzo and Giulia made those
bangin ass Italian sausages; he started coming here
too, Lorenzo, a few years ago after his first heart attack
back when he could walk in without the oxygen tank in
tow. This one boy who, just last week, strolled in dressed
down in all white on his way to this party at Broad, and
bad news Champloss is in need of penicillin again; he's
dragged in by a correctional officer; both of them, him
and the officer—a girl I went to high school with, rockin
late-in-life barrettes, who every teen and two gym teachers
called badd—were both coughing up a lung, just
back-throat spittin on everybody from the waiting room
and through the hallway, from the window to the walls
and past the egg-white cashier's counter, all together
makes me remember that one time she had burnt our
point guard and was like "my bad" in public to wild
laughter that lasted all year. That same year Sean Paul
and Busta Rhymes forever christened the colloquialism
for gettin burnt: make it clap; and this, the reclaiming
of our twenty-four-points-per-game averaging star's
pride would then take a back seat to a more historically
salient reenactment, because too soon after, this white
girl at an away game ran around askin everybody on
the court and in the bleachers if she could give them
head and, despite our best efforts, he gave in, needy

(what an obvious mistake), after which she informed her boyfriend down court that our point guard had raped her, thus vanishing our sports star into the system like my younger brother after he slapped the taste outta this teacher's mouth for choking him one Wednesday afternoon because he was three minutes late to his tenth-grade social studies class. They both left behind kids and girlfriends, one of whom, Tasha, is a nurse manager now, on her way out the door after a long night shift reminding me that my scrubs are "fuckin highwaters bro" and I remind her to mind her fuckin business and she says I love you too and I say that's why I'm not watchin ya bad ass kids no more—one of whom when sleeping over jumped from the top bunk into the ceiling fan at 2:43 a.m., cracking his head open and complaining afterward about his almost-but-not-quite ascension into Miles Morales—but she got a new boyfriend now who's apparently always dreamed of being a stay-at-home-dad-type nigga who I discovered only recently in our last text thread: a video of him, tall, fine, brown, in Reebok slides and "Every Nigga Deserves" sweater playin *Fallout* with the kids in her living room while she sat back rolling a blunt just outside on the patio, hummingbirds gathered around her hanging feeders in a scene that, if coupled with the right soundtrack, would have made me cry.

In the next room a skinny girl child with box braids got a toothache; she look like my sister a little, and I play peek-a-boo with her behind the curtain. Back and forth she finds it hilarious as I jump from round the corner and retreat, hit the corner and retreat. She's laughing. Another child's face is chewed off by a dog that was not, despite the popular assumptions of many of our straight-haired staff members, a pit bull. Fighting dogs considered, my uncle Red Top, who wore matching leather Thriller outfits and ran in gangs with my grandfather and serves somewhat of a mentor function to my father at Holmesburg and other State Road haunts, is two rooms away from the nurse's station dying of high blood pressure; it's so high this nigga might explode at any minute. Ever since my youth on the receiving end of grown men's knuckles I'd always wondered how they would die; decades of free therapy though, for better and worse at these universities, has obliterated my revenge fantasies and outward animosity, turned all righteous-or-not rage into flaccid Pokémon-style plushies, which is not the same as delimiting my curiosity; a more literal understanding of blood pressure, prior to my overeducation by those my advisor aptly calls the ruling class, was like that Jay-Z line in Mya's "Best of Me, Part 2": "Pain is pleasure and pressure bust pipes," which struck me as being about fucking and eating with equally infinite freedom, which is always the kind that hurts yourself and everybody else, the fantasies that rap music thrums through our tendons as I starve, in true exaggerating fashion, at work, as we all starve, like poor

Richard in perpetuity. Red Top is a Motown-only nigga though. An immortal of a certain era, I prefer he not die at all. This is selfish, I often think, capturing and compartmentalizing the pain of others into ways *I* might feel about it, patterns of thought and speech in the economics of morality, saying fuck it to whatever they might otherwise want or need since I'm the one collecting empathy with the book, reading books.

He's also an incredible liar though, Red Top, and as my link to an estranged father whose body, if I'm ever to write a worthwhile book, is also my archive, a story, I gotta hold on to that thing just before love, which is probably necessity. Red Top's been in good with the guards at Holmesburg for longer than anyone should be there at all. This is how he does it: As an ex-army medic, a fate we share however many generations apart, they saw him as trustworthy, the doctors and the scientists, the soldiers and guards and every celly rightfully suspicious of Johnson & Johnson or Dow Chemical; this meant if he was doing the skin tests, well, why shouldn't everyone else? He strolled around retrofitted with patches glued to non-wounds for twice the pay, hustling as an early influencer on the gospel of new shampoos and skin creams, soaps and detergents, conditioners, growth serums and microbial regulation ointments, the whole spectrum of human scientific capacity on display and waving the green flag of prosperity at anybody who wanted, well, needed, which was everyone, money on their books. He's a pirate with that leg long lost to diabetes and a fake eyepatch on the surface, suggesting his alliance with fellow inmates all the while collecting cash through the back door. Klingman might as well have christened the man himself; and yet, here he is, every week, still dying. Looking at him, I assume something of what the father, a figure I know little about, might be, and contemplate whether my psychic inquiries through Red Top on all the shit he did and was done to him are private affairs between my father and himself, niggas who all know they know, or whether I've earned the right to this information and its deployment through blood or history or wrongdoing or American make-believe. Though in the latter case we all seem to know too much already. He's my main source of stories for the story about the story these days. He's also tryna stay calm while screaming "Shut the fuck up! Shut the fuck up!" at the drunk soaked in piss beside him who calls me a bitch cause I said he couldn't have no more prune juice. And Louie the nurse is crackin up too, beside me now, and the dude calls him a fuckin spic—and I think *Weird, people still say that?*—and the both of us stand outside the curtain wagging fingers at this nigga like "Wow sir, that's why you bout to stay thirsty today wit ya lil thirsty ass." Next door a sickly high regular coming down from some new shit the kids are calling crocodile grabs at Anya's ass, her smacking his hand, him calling her a dirty worthless bitch for the improprieties of "no" and screaming at the top of his lungs all the ways he's been done wrong by the world and needs some pussy as recompense. I'm paraphrasing, of course, lots of things: the restrictions of narrative forms, a history, a people, a way of life, though fractured by the silliness of responsibilities like protecting the reader— from what, one wonders, if not simply the people I love? At my most desperate back in the teen years up before sunrise and down after the restaurant closed I used to pray for someone to protect us all from labor in every conceivable form, watching some dickhead on television deploy sixth-grade rhetoric concerning working families or the dignity of work and worse, the celebratory clapping after each empty phrase. Bombs exploding in the background.

This old head who cashes her checks at Ace Check Cashing across the street next to Dunkin Donuts, who always calls me Suga and says my mother did a great job raising me, is in the next room after the next room in need of a knee brace. Never would I shatter her illusion about who or what took responsibility for my upbringing because I might love her more than my actual mother. She recalls, and I can't remember nothin to contradict it, that when I was a baby she would talk to my mom and them when we was waitin outside the Salvation Army for paper bag lunches. This was before the era of Penn's Chinese store where, on the slimmest of funds, you could overdraw your account by $20.00 at

Citizens Bank and then take that twenty and eat rice and gravy for a whole week or so at a dollar fifty per platter. This is prolly not true, but them Salvation Army lines seemed shorter twenty or thirty years ago, and did it also just feel true that there was more food? And is this the appropriate form to question the progress espoused by my more literate peers as I look around at everyone getting hungrier?

"I don't know how it happened, Suga," she tells me as I unpack the Sam Splint and Ace Wrap, priming it, digging my fingers in to prefabricate a shape approximating comfort. "I was just walkin wit my hoagie and this dang curb came outta nowhere." Every day she be talkin about some curb that came outta nowhere, like the curbs be stalkin her, creeping up from the sewer on her jaunts to the market. She's my favorite patient today and two days ago and the day before that. Always something different: a strange mole, low blood sugar, sprained ankle, carpal tunnel. She's a courtroom scribe up Fifteenth and Arch, the building that to this day inspires in me tachycardia at the slightest glance or drive-by, and a panic attack twice. How embarrassing. I like the way she says Suga but hate when younger women call me that. She got the hoagie from Wilson's, the superior option, not that garbage ass Olney Steak and Beer, where, several years before, a man who looks to me like the man who strangled and shot my ganny, beat Eraina Merritt, mother of four, unconscious and raped her. My friend Merv, before he killed himself, called that place, Olney Steak and Beer that is, "super regular," coining thereafter a description for all underwhelming food up to and exceeding the "overprominent social form of the cold cut writ large," and the oodles n noodles my son makes with no soup and way too much salt, the class-crossing comparison to what some folks might call "mid."

I am myself, starving, waitin for Ray to pick me up something from Wilson's and have been waitin a little too long honestly. He comes by Broad and Olney all the time for reasons I will never truly understand or to take pictures or on his way to some woman's house who hired him to take pictures or on his way back from some woman's house who hired him to take pictures and after seeing him in person has since decided to indulge in a little well-fed pretty-boy dick. This nigga refuses to try for a driver's license again even though he might finally afford a car, dedicating himself instead to the unpredictable rank and randomish violence of the Broad Street line subway. Because of this, or a lifetime of hypervigilance tilted over the edge by our deployment to Iraq, Ray "stay strapped," even though he don't even fuckin talk like that in real life. And back in Baghdad Ray and I used to make fun of the white boy's obsession with guns, especially the AK-47s, those old and boringly mass-produced 7.74 round slinging clunky kind of murderous memorabilia, hanging then from the shoulder slings and wood

9

grain mantles of half the snow honkeys who made it past our first year home; we was mad as hell havin to carry and clean the things as part of our paycheck and health insurance but here these fuckers was, collecting them and posing in they brown bloomers, freshly stolen phalluses, sending the pictures to god knows who—perhaps the K–12 teachers they'd impregnate and start families with, the parade of semiqueer thirtysomethin West Philly social workers tryna save us, random round the way girls later left widows to the suicides—as if we were occupying some kind of paradise, a baby Eden down the street from home with camel spiders and a touchable landscape and, after finding out camel spiders weren't even really spiders anyway, solpugids apparently, much to my own disappointment, I'd lost all hope in discovery, in developing a true taxonomy of the world as it is, was, or could be, according to the experts. Ray once killed a camel spider and put it on our platoon sergeant's seat right before a mission brief; the man almost died of a terror that, by then, everybody had long since got used to, the all night every night searching for bombs.

SOMETIMES I FORGET WHICH tense I'm supposed to be in though, and struggle remaining compliant to forms of disciplinarity which shelter us from reality, but often open up into better things, like contingent employability.

If there are subjects, objects, and verbs, why not just put them in that order forever as if the main provenance of transferring thought and feeling to page were to convey information, glancing around at all the good such things have done. More importantly though, this is not a story about me. But I do have the flu, I think. Or something. Or it don't matter. And it might be impossible for me to tell yall the truth, the whole truth and nothin but the story, story, story—where beginnings, middles and ends are concerned, the sweet Western satisfaction of triumphant conclusions, which really means inclusion in the world—without fuckin up what little proximity to freedom we might otherwise eke out, so imma say what I can, when possible, given certain profound constraints both external and interior, those anticipations, the ways they've long since made me me. As my homegirl Aisha always say, *You gotta stop tellin everybody everything all the damn time.*

Red Top asks me what I been up to, and says they proud of me, but he don't know why I'm still wearing this "gay ass nail polish," to which I normally respond "What, they don't let yall niggas look nice in prison?" I don't know who *they* are in either instance, but I kind of do, and hate both amalgamation and assumption even though I do both all the time as a requirement for communication. I'm reminded that everybody seems to be proud of something. He wanna know about my kids, how big they got, if they still alive. I'm stuck in family court, which I'd recently recognized as worse than a war zone by any measure in every measure; I am stuck sending videos and Facetiming in perpetuity when they're with me—either half or all of the time—scanning the environment to prove there are no immediate threats and copious running water, stuck in a form of interruption regarding what I could be to them in some other history, wading through work or play or caretaking under constant surveillance and the threat of incarceration, which the courts are only able to see as an ex-lover's continued devotion to the almighty figure of the child.

The Old One, GodRex96, don't like me no more, thinks I'm too hard on him, and he may be right; the world is hard on him in ways that obliterate his sensitivities; I just want him to clean up after himself: clothes off the floor and ravioli cans outta the bathroom cabinet, next to the Crest, above the African body oil they sell for $2.99 at the hair store. Be nice, please, I beg him. The Long One, QueenWolf9k, is emerging from her shell; I voluntold her to be in the Seussical Jr. and she was like "See, this what Whitney Houston mom did to her and that didn't work out good"—however, she's no longer shy to sing and is making progress with her voice instructor though her mom won't help pay for it, or anything for that matter, nor can the child be willed to clean her room. The Ravagers, BumblebeeFort, and GodRaptor69 hardly live in this universe, strangling the dogs and burying our cat in clothes, harassing the easily rousable GodRex96 by making hideous paper puppets and knocking on his door like "This you! Hahahaha!" and mocking him in a brooding tone that suggests an awkward sophistication which is admirable, since these people have just learned language in the first place. A twinge of pride shatters me at the punch line of every well-organized joke, a single tear dropping into the grease as I fry the chicken and they circle the kitchen asking "Is it done yet? Is it done yet?" like I'm not just as hungry tryna crisp the bird to excellence in the cast-iron, blocking out their wails rather than under-cook or burn the juicy thighs and drumsticks, my eyes set squarely on the thick one at the back left corner of the pan, shimmering gold, the blood popping from its little skin pocket where I sliced it open to investigate. Once, while driving, BumblebeeFort asked if we all knew what sound a pterodactyl makes and after receiv-ing a flurry of resolute or confused "nos" he was like "brrrrllllluuuu!" And it stuck. We have no choice but to believe it now. At night, pending behavioral reports from the school and whether or not people decide to put their clothes on after bathing or to run around the house ass naked plopping tiny wet mudprints across the floor, screaming and wrestling for an hour—and yes, here is where sometimes people consider beating children—we play *Sackboy: A Big Adventure* on the living room PS5, where I dress down in sequin octopus regalia running, jumping, hopping, swinging and climbing and dying at the head of the crew, QueenWolf9k focused, GodRex96 frustrated, GodRaptor69 fucked up on some wall or dead and BumblebeeFort confused about where his stark-naked Sackboy, who looks exactly like him in real life, that delicious shade and texture of black baby brown, can even be located on the map.

I tell Red Top a version of the truth wrapped in a longer lie and say them kids are fine and ask him what the fuck is up with his blood pressure. Some of the nurses say it's the highest they ever seen. They don't know how he's alive. Red Top, member of the living dead, 1.2 acres of skin and only somewhat of a mule.

"You know Black here too," he says. "So is Mom. They up on the eighth floor, cutty." It's the sixth floor, but I don't correct him. I like how older black men in my life say "cutty" all the time as their filler word, now transformed into "jawn" or "nigga" for us.

A gun drops from the waistline of a boy in the bay who's bleeding to death. The tourniquet I tighten around his thigh and all the blood, so much blood we pump into him seems like a waste of time. His girlfriend is crying. There are brown paper bags around them, some soaked red, some filled with his clothes and another with a bunch of crumpled-up ducats he had on him.

"Niggas be tryna commit suicide," my friend D, another ED tech, says. "Fuck would you be just strollin around North Philly with that much money on you? Askin for it."

"Maybe he was planning to buy a big lunch," another nurse says.

"Yeah, Temple can't gentrify that fast, nigga," D replies. "Thought it was sweet."

A doctor comforts his crying girlfriend while the police ask questions. Some of the questions go unanswered. I think about what it means to die of natural causes, or really feel natural or get to decide what is natural or unnatural and under what circumstances and in whose language, as I return to Red Top's room. Red Top does not think this is important to think about. On the PlayStation app, I receive an alert about QueenWolf9k downloading *Stray*, *Spirit of the North*, *The Witcher*, and five lesser-known titles before school. I text her like Oh hey cutie watcha doing? You all ready for school? No response. Then, she writes, I can't believe we got trashed like that dadda. She means the night prior in *Diablo* where the demon Astaroth thrashed our motley crew of three—Me as Barbara the Barbarian, her as Yunix the Druid, Godrex96 as Vergil the Necromancer—for three hours straight as we ducked, dodged and slammed health potions chipping away infinitesimally at a health bar that might as well have been the racial mountain and yelling to each other from across the room "Revive me!" or "Why is boul so diesel?!" or "Daddy you gotta increase the play time for the day, we got logged out!"

Anyway, "You must be gettin all the pussy around

here," Red Top says. I check his blood pressure again. Off the charts.

"Well, looks like you bout to die, old nigga," I say. He laughs at this, so we both laugh. He wants to know if I'm married. If imma go upstairs and talk to his mom, my great-grandmother, not by blood but relation. I don't know what I could possibly tell her, from one world to another. I walk away from his room, toward one of the elevated desks on either side of the nurse's station where I normally write between patients, over the moans and yelling, amidst the demands that I do anything but this. Red Top flings his remote call bell at another patient who won't shut up, not realizing it's tied down, so it yo-yos back and knocks him in the temple.

A ND SO WHEN I found this crack in the foundation of my job's labor practices—that I would only be flagged for working over sixteen hours straight if it was within the same unit—I figured myself best suited to the emergency department, my home station; Med Surg, where I got my start as a nurse aide; and of course, the always understaffed ICU, where some of my favorite nurses, like Tierra, were always shopping for bullshit and grindin niggas up at the nurse's station or stuck in the middle of a code. I enjoy the lack of in-betweens there in the ICU, the proximity to black-and-white standards like in the ED, that whole "hurry up and wait" vibe that reminds me of the army. When I roll up to Med Surg with an admission, Ms. Johnson's third time this week, everybody's like *Ain't you supposed to be on this floor later?* And I'm dodging the question cause the nurse manager here is weirdly intense and a bit of a snitch generally.

One of them middle management types watching your pockets like that check is subtracted straight from their check and not the throwaway change from some family who own the hospital network anyway and probably owned both your great-grandparents too, one of whom is still alive, wheezing to death in a double room next door with no privacy. Ms. Johnson is alive but knocked out, and I've been around too long to get antsy tryna lift dead weight solo; it makes my back hurt even considering it. So soon as I see Lise walk by I call on her for help transferring. Lise being another person who was in the army before this, and was therefore socialized into a kind of teamwork radically uncommon in the most liberal of civilian workforces. Ray thinks she's abhorrent because she doesn't read and has a bunch of kids; she thinks Ray is shallow and pretentious, all language with no heart or experience otherwise; I think Ray is a hypocrite since the only reason he doesn't have children is the financial, legal, and political matrix that has made abortions safe and legal in Philadelphia for those with roughly $600.00 and the happenstance of sexual partners who don't want no kids either, at least not with him.

I knew Lise before the army, but hardly. We'd deployed in adjacent years, and she was in Afghanistan. We'd only met because of the hospital; it fostered one kind of social life at the expense of another. While Lise was deployed, she had to give full custody of her son and daughter to Isiah, who then was either not working or underemployed. They didn't have a great deal of beef at the time, but there was little beyond the generalizable reasons for being together, that most people could never afford otherwise. Of course, while Lise was getting shot at and blown up and yes, maybe or maybe not fucking a fine ass interpreter who looked like an older sibling of Sameer Gadhia, her words not mine, alongside her *Shut the fuck up you woulda did it too* when I chuckled, Isiah was balling out in a 2022 Dodge Charger. All the kids who deployed had one, and so did Isiah despite the fact that he couldn't enlist because he never passed the physical fitness test. Every dime that Lise earned was not enough, and so she came back broke to Isiah who, rather than use the money she'd sent for the Montessori school around the corner, made it rain at Set It Off on Second and Cambria and left the kids with his mom, or home alone (if they were already asleep) and brought back no fewer than seventeen women to the house with the kids in the other room. My first question was, of course, *How could this nigga leave the Ring camera on?* Me and Cee and Ray together got up $11k for Lise to get right, like we did for Cee when his mom went swag surfin on his labor out in Vegas and the child support almost got him locked up. Ray suggested that we kill Isiah, but he was too serious and rash about it, so everybody dropped it. I ended up a witness in Lise's custody fight when she came back, as she would later be in mine.

This nigga Isiah showed up in black-and-white Adidas slides and Jordan sweatpants. I didn't even know they sold them jawns no more, those relics from the reign of Foot Locker, with the Jump Man right next to the left pocket. They were red. Lise's lawyer, who was also my lawyer, this light-skin old head who does kickboxing, is on his second divorce and, though affordable, if that means anything in this context, is mid-tier homophobic—like, if my own family is a 9/10, he's around a 4/10, says, in reference to my earrings, gait or nail polish, things like "Well you know, it's okay if you do, it doesn't bother me" mostly unprompted—turned to her and was like "Is this nigga wearing sweatpants?" And started laughing. Turns out the laughter was unwarranted though, because despite Isiah's lack of attorney, extreme belligerence, yelling, being cut off at the edge of threats, the admittance to beating the kids because they wouldn't go to sleep, and his clear disinterest in their education, or anything interior to them for that matter excluding the canned phrase "I takes care of my kids," and god I hate niggas who say that, he was awarded joint custody. Lise went to pop the trunk. It made sense to me. She'd kept a shotgun at home, but moved around the world with a black beretta like all the medics and officers had, a comfort item, like a Snuggie, wrapped tight around her person in the form of possibility, in the form of *fuck outta here* or *okay, okay, imma be right back*, a ghastly knowing tucked into the soul like your toddler's teething ring or the religion you're born into, an actual factual that if worse came to worst she could make it even worse.

But her lawyer was more levelheaded. He had sense, and patience, the patience and the sense of having done this a million times, he claimed, straightening out his slightly-too-wide suit. "He bout to fuck this up very quickly. Dude is clearly a dickhead. Just be patient, and we'll make sure to get you that full custody because this nigga is a narcissist. He don't really wanna take care of them kids. He wanna control you. Don't let him."

Sure enough, clip still full half a year later, Lise was awarded full custody. Isiah had missed dozens of drop-offs and pickups and doctor's appointments. Had cursed and screamed in front of the police station, though that still wasn't enough. It was the fact that he'd left the kids at his friend's house where their son was molested, if that's the right word, the details of which Lise has decided never to explicate any further. Her son, SupaKiller89, was afraid to tell her and so told me after reading an essay I'd written about being raped as a child (just like everybody else and they mom we knew) so then I told her, which he took as a betrayal and I felt was a necessity. And so, she found it hard to celebrate the inevitable full custody order and the subsequent support of $489.00 monthly from Isiah who, for his part, was not at all apologetic and still in every way a complete dickhead. At most, he'd said that his young boul would be good, *all he did was get his dick wet with a fine ass old head, he lucky.* At the time, Lise and I were sleeping together, all our kids in the next room piled on bunk beds knocked out in front of that diabolical program *Paw Patrol* and she cried a lot, and I was not, I'd later discover, but sure as hell felt, more horrible than any paragon of my gender at comforting her. She would be crying and simultaneously upset that we weren't fucking, annoyed at my attempts to talk, tugging at my dick like some unbreakable toy, and I'd thought it inappropriate to try through the crying, despite my sociobiological imperative to initiate and, while I didn't tell her this then, I'd also started Trazodone which destroyed me, was making me gain weight too fast and had my shins aching; I couldn't run anymore for sport or reprieve, and though still horny, I was more interested in taking my own life—broke and having people demand things from me and dreaming of the life insurance money the kids would get and having been caught with my own beretta pressed against my temple outside my apartment by the older Antiguan lady who always walks her little Pomskys down our street any old time of night, complaining randomly how the red snapper here is trash—I was not at all able to get my dick hard, least of all the way Lise wanted, with a firmness that irrevocably proved my desire for her, which in a sociohistorically manipulative chain of events would consequently open up her desire for me. I did eventually tell her I was depressed and she said duh, so is everybody that's not really an excuse. And this felt true. So we mostly drank together after I ate her out and feigned arousal and forced an additional intimacy on top of, and instead of learning to trust what intimacy was already there until the point that, with serious advisement from our collective friendships, we simply stopped fucking. A week later Lise was spitting in my mouth as I came before hopping off and squirting onto my bedsheets and laughing like *I'm not washin those.* A week after that I was soft again and she was pregnant, already swallowing the pill and saying we should just be friends; she'd moved in with somebody else, at least for a couple of months until she got bored and bounced so now they share custody of the next kid and an ugly puggle named Strom Thurmond. The new nigga don't like Isiah neither, but more importantly he's a very good fourth teammate in *Diablo.*

SupaKiller89 did, however, start speaking to me again, or rather, to Indalecio Lantis, my *Final Fantasy XIV* persona when the new expansion dropped; being a Black Mage on one's own would be too hard, survival too limited. A school of us, all Black Mages, tore through the wyverns of Heavensward, SupaKiller89 trying out new dance macros on Leviathan's beached corpse and saying Uncle Joe can I see your spell list setup? And Do people actually use manafont? All the while exuding confidence to the core alliance, a damage dealer in the back mostly talking shit but puttin up numbers. Despite my getting kicked out of several savage raids for my confusion, not attacking or sleeping, or dragging the right monster at the right time, SupaKiller89 never lost faith in me. Not quick enough to type he would call or text and wanna stay on the phone the whole time, trash talkin the other people in our group or describing to me which characters he thought were cute in real life, mostly boys, tepid, in a way that, without clear sanction, let me know not to tell his mother this time. Folks online always thought he was older, though I could never see what they saw, his text always sounding the way he looked as a baby, his avatar, an older black woman with white locs exemplifying the too-familiar and impossible amalgam of mother and lover most of us longed for, coaxing it out of the women in our sphere or otherwise overrepresenting our imaginations as reality, a consequence of our unfinished forebears and that necessary love, that forceful love, that elegant and deeply painful love otherwise foreclosed to us by the world.

BUT THERE ARE PLENTY of other reasons to love Lise, imagination aside. Practical: She's one of three people in here as tall as me, so we can transfer patients safely at adult height without further destroying our bodies. Hustle: Lise also got kids and is in school, so she's also always in here, sliding through whatever department will have her. Hater: Lise is a hater, but the proper kind, not the variety who fucks with your money. She has two exes in the department: Tierra and Isiah, the latter who we've both wished on various occasions would at least get beat the fuck up or his mouth bust open or, at the very least, manifest the collective dream that someone rip off that damn eyebrow ring. Every time she brings up Tierra it starts with "this bitch," either endearingly or in a murderous rage; whenever this nigga Isiah comes up, it usually leads to a commiseration about the failings of family court and the never-ending inquiry of who the hell is actually benefiting from such an institution because it sure as hell ain't nobody we know.

Regarding the goings-on of labor, as if there was anything else, I really appreciate Lise because the tales of inquiring for help from one of the other CNAs or nurses up here are wild generally, but among the most mundane responses is a "Hold on" while a teammate runs into the bathroom for forty-five minutes, an "Okay, lemme page so-and-so," while a nigga waits online for Jordans dropping or Beyoncé tickets or, up to and including a scenario requiring the utmost urgency—is her heart rate supposed to be that low?—a sly ass "Well you're big and strong, baby, I'm sure you can lift her," from an older married woman who, all other things being equal, you may or may not have had sex with before, who now sends you random black history factoids on social media unsolicited between nudes, the way young people do with memes, as if this constitutes a discourse. This term, a term Lise hates: "discourse," yes, but also things like "intercourse" more so or "have sex with" or "sleep with" are terms Ray loves. *Have sex with, Why don't you just say "fuck"?* Lise says; I've had to deal with her clowning before and in the aftermath of this affair, all her "I told you so nigga," and the bouncing off singing "Heartbreak Hotel" into the break room. And it's true, homegirl might have gotten the best of me a little bit, the way Jay-Z was tryna get Mya, and perhaps I really did think she was gonna leave her husband or didn't care or trained myself not to care given what kind of relation was available at the time.

"This bitch Tierra told me," Lise says, raising the bed to our height, "this bitch Tierra told me you two clowns bout to go to Belize together." *Together*, I think, is a strong word.

I don't say anything about the bathing suit choices I'm currently being spammed with from the floor below us. They are, in fact, bedazzling, even the monocolor one-pieces. Instead, I'm like "Yeah, you tryna come?"

"Yall get on my fuckin nerves," she says. "'You tryna come?'" she repeats in a mousy dickhead voice, mocking me, knowing damn well she can't come.

We untuck the sheets from under Ms. Johnson's stretcher, fold her arms over her chest, wrap her nice like an old lady burrito instinctively, and get ready to slide her over into bed.

"I know yall ain't takin them kids," Lise says.

"Fuck them kids," I say. GodRex96 and Queen-Wolf9k both texting me in our group chat pictures of cartoon giraffes all day like daddy, this you? and I'm responding whenever I can like ain't you little fuckers supposed to be doing school work? Little assholes swear they funny but don't never answer the phone when it's important. Make sure yall walk the dogs when you get home, love you too, I text in a response to this still of Farigiraf that says in purple lettering: "Hi I'm the new evolution of daddy!"

Between us all, Lise, Tierra and I, there are ten children under the age of twelve. And while Tierra and I share custody, begrudgingly or not, with other people: her with two semidomesticated hood niggas and me with three different women: one who is mostly absent, another of whom is more hood than any hood nigga I ever met—solidifying an intense friendship littered with asterisks and caveats—and another who, while ceaselessly kind to her children, poses a consistent threat to my freedom in the register of care, Lise ain't seen an unqualified moment away from her kids since the custody fight with Isiah; despite Terrell now taking his own baby most of the time, there's nowhere she can trust with the rest of them.

"Truly. Fuck them kids," Lise says. "Them spoiled ass kids. They wit ya mom tonight or they mom? I saw you tryna be slick and grab like twenty hours today."

I haven't told Lise yet about my own mom smoking crack in the apartment with the kids while I was at work, my taking the deepest breaths ever and tryna stay calm as I rolled up to the toddlers out front with the dogs, grape jelly all over the counter and floor and the big kids zombified by TV. Far as she knows, Mom's been sober for the longest stretch in history, three months. I don't say how this makes me feel a bit like a child again, like the past nineteen years of day-in day-out grinding hadn't meant shit because with my own mistakes and failures, the world, and a set of increasing desires for nice things combined I was basically back at square one. Or at least this is how my body feels, my body that, despite its best efforts, will not stop being a body. Mom was walking around in a state, opening windows and casting suspicions at the air which, I've come to feel in my adult life, are real suspicions about what real people want to do to her body, a collapsing of whispers and pin pricks killing her not so softly that, despite their inability to be heard by everyone should, nonetheless, never be felt so acutely by my children as they were by me at the tender age of six, sitting on the floor and wishing we could all die faster. I took the dogs and the twins in, those goofy little creatures whose main words were then still just "diddy" and "nom nom" and "eat eat" and "mommom," struggling not to yell, and called her an Uber. No shame about the event though, more how I responded, since Lise had the same exact shit happen with her dad when she got off work like three weeks ago. Walked into the house to him loopy and that smell you can never unknow. I'd seen him on the ave just languishing, high as shit, but I hadn't found the right time to bring it up, knowing already that of course, of course, she knew.

"They all with the new babysitter," I say. "But The Old One's mom gonna pick him up later, she in town for a funeral—'"

Lise shakes her head. "How long you think this one bout to last?" she says. "And how much it cost?"

\* \* \*

LISE AND I HAD shared a sitter for a while, who died in a car accident. After that, I'd had a string of them that left because it was too much on top of their full-time gigs or they weren't doin nothin except letting the kids watch TV while they drank rosé and downloaded PlayStation games in the living room. All I tell Lise is that it isn't worth it unless you get a few hours overtime, which she also already knows. We roll Ms. Johnson from one side to the other, getting rid of her green ED blankets and laying her flat on the white Med Surg sheets to discover, of course, of course, that everything old and new is already soiled. Soiled prolly being an understatement. I mean, in this case the brown and wet is already seeping into the mattress and I'm glad for two things just then, one being that I asked Lise in particular to come and help, and the other that Ms. Johnson is still out of it because she gets so embarrassed when this happens, and really getting her clean before she wakes up will feel like a certain kind of mercy, a pleasure of which, I'm told, I sometimes take too seriously. My back hurts, so we pause a bit and I crack it a few times, my stomach growling at the exposure as I bend back.

"You old as shit," Lise says. "And nasty." Then she looks at all the shit pooling and then over at me. "But don't get too excited. I know how you get."

I should explain.

There are just so few legal, attainable pleasures in life, so few tasks to be easily or fully completed in one's own lifetime that cleanliness, and no, not next to godliness, but maybe, whatever, depends on who you ask, cleanliness has become more satisfying than perhaps it should be. The pleasures of a clean home, my advisor might say, unmatched. She is correct. But you know what's even more pleasurable? Even more unmatched? Distributing a clean asshole. The pleasures of cleaning so thoroughly, so exactingly, someone who cannot do so for themselves. Really taking one's time and getting into the crevices, the butt holes, under the balls and titties, underarms, back fat and fupas, tender flesh creases behind the kneecaps, inside the crusty ears and under the fingernails, between those emaciated flaps of flesh, into the sunken jowls and worn-down shoulder pockets. Everything; I want it all. This same pleasure I've gotten washing my dirty ass little children in the tub, those people who, no matter how many times I say no, go walloping in the mud like ducks, dredging up shit and piss and insects, those people with whom, after a long day road tripping to the park or the beach or the lake, I find ecstasy just sliding some hypoallergenic wipes across their smooth ass brown baby booties and dipping them in the tub with some bath bombs and melatonin bubble bath for the kill. All the giggles and wacky baby fish movement and holding my hand under their slick stomachs as they paddle and tell me that yes, due to this bathtub experience they do in fact know how to swim better than baby shark and beyond the deepest and bluest ocean of LL Cool J's wildest imagination. All this despite dragging me into the depths of the five-foot neighborhood pool kicking and wailing every summer, choking me to death talkin bout "Daddy I can swim better on your back!" Lyin ass kids. But also, I reminisce about the giant tubs at the rehab center where I'd worked before, all Miyazaki *Spirited Away* style scrubbing the fuck outta this big black dude named George who used to be a scuba diver telling me all about Belize and whale sharks and shit, surprised at his experience scuba diving I'm like damn, I really gotta go see the world. Felt basic, like here I was at this hospital honing in on wiping ass and there's this dude from my neighborhood who was once a professional scuba instructor in Belize and everybody at that job thought he was just some crazy soft hood nigga who was too fat for care and couldn't take care of himself and come to find out this nigga had a whole wife who was one of the first black judges in Philly—whom we later discovered I served at my old job before that, the retirement home—and lived to be almost a hundred watching their two daughters get married before she died, all the while these two loving each other to death and George just flat-out crying sometimes and saying he misses her when his daughters visit they all cry and I cry in my car most often, thinking about this and seeing George and seeing the only people I know in the hospital and the prisons on State fucking Road. And my dad and uncles are there long term with Mom and Ganny in and out and siblings on the way in ways that feel consistently grievable but far beneath the register of event or popular politics which might otherwise make martyrs out of them and solidify their place in the liberal order as persons. But *this* shit I can do something about, the shit gunked into the creases of George's elbows or bathing Ms. Johnson's body and tucked away in the pockets of their wounds all bloody and weeping, *that* shit I can do something about, and do it well.

Lise be actin like she not into it, but this same person who drop her kids off at my house talkin bout "Can you just wash them up and put em in bed, I'll be right back" so she can go get some ass around the corner and half the time she butts in front of me to bathe them all at once before dashing out late to the booty call; having been trained on the same floor I know damn well every time a patient in Med Surg is thoroughly bussed with a little bit of sparkle sparkle, it's definitely her because it damn sure ain't Olivia or Jade or Jay or none of them. To my point, she's already letting the water get warm, whistling "Buy U a Drank" to herself—in the Tiny Desk tempo no less—and busting open soap packets in the big pink tub, the one for washing, not that little spit basin the lazier folks woulda snatched up in a hurry. I roll the shitty blanket under Ms. Johnson's side, wiping a little of the feces from her hips, from her waist as gently as I can, pained at the more normative and parallel scenario in which someone gazes upon such a mess and scratches across her skin with dry towels, smearing shit all over her and maybe, on a good day, deciding to change the top sheet if more than sixty percent soiled, the petty calculations of a care worker unable to imagine a plight worse than one's own punching the clock. Lise hands me the soapy bucket and turns Ms. Johnson on her other side.

"You wanna hook ya girl up?"

And I do. I'm soaking the white rag in our pink bucket and wringing it out just so, letting it cool down a little so it doesn't burn Ms. Johnson's skin. Around the bed sores I scrub in mini magic circles, feeling the dry clunks from the last time she was "cleaned" grow soft and fall off, with another towel dabbing the shit out of her sores, some healing and others putrid, on the verge of consuming her whole body. Every few scrubs or wipes I tuck the towel into the blanket and secure a new one, fold the blanket tighter under her, securing the clean flesh and revealing more of the soiled.

Rinsing. Repeating.

Lise wants to know who came up with the Belize idea.

"Both of us, kind of," I say. "You know she always be on vacation." Which was a version of the truth. Every other day Tierra was gettin flown out somewhere. She works four or five doubles in a row, stacks money, spends a few days with the kids and then a few days in Paris, Moscow, Turkey, Japan, Indonesia. Fendi-bag-wearing home-girls, some flight attendants, others models or married rich stacked in her photos and Instagram mentions. I had said jokingly, in a comment on one such photo of her in Bora Bora with her same day one crew, or some rich nigga which—to my surprise was not flagged for content—"Damn, you just out here, I'm tryna get like you." To which she responded by liking said comment and DMing me, "You play too much." I was not aware, but I kinda was aware that perhaps I played too much. But this was no longer a joking matter.

We started chatting more then, above and beyond the mandatory flirtations demanded of a hospital work day, which are only even about sex half the time, more than the casual invite out to the bar when she and Lise and a couple other work people went out, up to the point where she started hitting me up when her shifts got canceled at 3:00 a.m. and just saying, not asking, just saying, that she was comin over. Otherwise obliterated by the carefully constructed coyness of human romantic interaction in the field of gender—even by, and especially with progressives—her aggression perhaps was the most significant point of infatuation for me: immediate, forceful, needing. I might finally rest in pleasure, rather than endure the unpaid internship of small talk and overcast interest, the terrible expensive meals and malfeasance which pleases, somehow, too many of us as a social norm, the time lost for thinking under the aspirational tyranny of the couple form, the blind assumptions regarding what I might want or need, and the confidence that for my alleged being—negro male with interest in women—these were things so obvious they need never be questioned, far too many answers having been provided in blood by my forefathers or the semiotic inverse of Christina Aguilera's "What a Girl Wants" thrumming through the subconscious of millions of innocents gagging on the concerns of boys and men under the guise of universality which, in the end, hasn't left anybody close to whole or nearer an articulation of true desire. Desperate to quit something or die trying I deleted the apps, just happy to lie there on my back.

Having grown out of, so I thought, an impulse to shave years from my life span red-eyeing for sex, the fact that I might remain silent or simply say yes kept me saying *yes* and waking nonfunctional the next day more times than I could count. She sleeps hot and writhes around and, sensing my getting hard again, will laugh, lazily rubbing me against her until I can't stand it anymore, mocking me like "I thought you was too tired" and putting her hand on my chest, turning our bodies over to ride me. Tierra moves with practiced and gentle excitement. She uses her left hand, with the rose tattoo, having pressed the other palm on my beard and pulls me inside quicker than expected; I almost cum too fast, so she slows down with her legs wrapped around my waist till temperate, loosening, because she likes me to play with her clit while inside her, gesturing for spit on her chest and often joking "Not the face, not the face"; and when she cums this way, my knees buckle too, falling into her. She complains, rolling me off her body with a grunt, "You way heavier than you look boy," and puts me in her mouth as I try not to squirm as the last of everything leaves my body forever. I forget time and time again that there's a world outside of those nights, never washing my sheets when she leaves, knowing she'll be gone by morning and already waiting for her return pending the nights at her son's dad house or getting flown out.

But also, Belize had been on my bucket list.

I had this teacher once, while studying biology, who had a lab in Belize. A lab in Belize seemed like the most outrageous thing I'd heard of at the time, that there were people who studied biology and, since whale sharks migrate through Belize between March and June, she needed a station there, while also teaching at a U.S. university that was paying well above a living wage which, at the time, say, over ten years ago, was still numerically possible. We were breeding drosophila flies in the biology lab when she mentioned this casually, when I discovered that she, my teacher who touched a lot when addressing me, who had only moved from Prague two years ago, had a beach house lab in Belize. Breeding flies was much easier than I thought it would be, probing

and manipulating their tiny bodies with my burgeon-
ing god hands reminded me of the final boss in *Super
Smash Bros.*—those giant white gloves grasping, smacking, smashing and strangling whatever little avatar you
confront them with. We were cataloging genetic shifts
in eye color and wing mutations in the drosophila over
several generations inside a warm fridge as I imagined
the warmth of my teacher's home who lived in Northeast Philly. After our first date and this sloppy and gra-
tuitous kind of kissing outside a movie theater—this, a
few days after I'd received a string of long emails from a
personal address, having nothing to do with biology lab
proper—I discovered that she lived with her boyfriend
but was, to no one's surprise, disappointed with the mal-
aise of the relationship; it seemed those overdosed flies
in the infinite Tsukuyomi-like sleep were the corollary
to middle-class folks of a certain age and era just falling
into sleepy TV marriages and then climbing into bed,
well, in this case, the front seat of a red Pontiac Grand
Prix, with students or whoever was available, though
in my mind, I know, I know, I was no student. I was a
grown ass man who'd fallen in love in lieu of power with
a smart and beautiful woman whose own world didn't
conform immediately to the given world I was otherwise at war with, or I was horny and lonely enough to
ride this fantasy till the wheels fell off, or her real boyfriend started emailing me, whichever came first, in
this case it was the former. Though she'd refused to let

me in her house and proposed oral each night in the front seat of said Grand Prix we eventually fucked once in the adjunct office with no condom on a rolling chair without arm rests as a sort of goodbye, I guessed. I had to appreciate that she was the first and only person at a university not to treat me like a complete idiot and held me to a high standard in class, saying we could never see each other outside if I got anything less than an A on a test. And while I took pride in never responding to her boyfriend's emails, which ranged from mild condescension to threat level orange, I did in fact receive my first B+ ever that spring at the beginning and end of my college career in biology.

But why rehearse this at all with Lise, she already know, in grad school as she is now and talking about the vertigo and those people from the other America so often and even though we share damn near everything without reservation I've never talked about sex with Tierra and neither has she, even though I get these long ass parables from every no-good baby-dick good-for-nothing bitch nigga or down-low dependent hoe whose apartment or grandmama's apartment she come slinking out of at whatever time of night while me and her kids watching *Fullmetal Alchemist* on the big screen between three dogs and a misguided cat. Those nights we sometimes stay up too late too, drinking that nasty ass rosé she likes and complaining about family court again or laughing at things we can't say or feel in public.

On those nights The Long One, always tryna be up late in grown folks' business, snuggles up on Lise like she's her mom and always asks her, without fail, when she's coming back.

WE'RE MOSTLY DONE WASHING and rinsing Ms. Johnson, and Lise smacks me in the face with the balled-up new sheets.

"Thanks," I say, my stomach growling.

"You're welcome," she says. "You sound hungry."

It's obvious, I am hungry if nothing else, the way Lloyd Banks was on that first album. It's hard to think of anything else, daydreaming about that time the Jehovah Witness lady from Pleasure Platters delivered three trays of king crab legs to the break room before they closed to competition from Uber Eats. My glasses fall off, and when I bend down to pick them up with an awkward combination of elbow and clean pinky finger I drop my phone too, so I scan a bunch of missed calls and texts from my mom at another new number, which mostly indicates her being quite high and asking me to bring her some soft pack Kools and money and if I still have my gun—which reminds me I've left it in my work locker—because she needs me to kill someone; the texts from Tifah are telling me she needs more child support—which is only $250.00 a month plus $28.00 in arrears since The Long One lives with me—and this is technically in response to my clinically scripted inquiry from three weeks ago about whether she plans on seeing The Long One as it's been several months of their absolute distance but several years since I'd gotten help with child care, clothes or food; Myra is suggesting the twins move to the school that costs $52,000.00 a year per child instead of the new "better than Philly though not white neighborhood" school by me all the while reminding me, as a courtesy, that she can return to court for more money and I will have *less* time, and that there's another problem with my insurance, which costs $830.00 a month for the family, and that $1,400.00 a month in support is fair for now but we gotta look again when their school starts and can I take them to the dentist in an hour? She'd made the appointment a few months ago, and if I do not comply or text back within thirty minutes it will not be pretty and there is a selfie of her smiling in my favorite sundress with the kids in the background from the last time they went to the farmer's market and it ends with let me know if you would like to come over for dinner with us on Friday and my last thing is that you need to watch your mouth in front of the children, and keep them away from the lude and horrific things you listen to and watch on television as they are starting to mimic you and your racial insensitivities and blatant chauvinism are going to show up in my children as I have already been alerted a great many times about these problems from their teachers and I will be saving this for our next meeting; Alicia, drunk and horny, had sent me titty pictures last night, assumedly cause the first couple niggas was busy but I'd stopped embarrassing myself with her after she'd changed her roster to fucking the married neighbor in hiding over me due to the fact that I was annoying, asking her about her life too much which was what I'd been taught she wanted, he was "less annoying," with a "marginally larger dick," but I was also "welcome to try back some other times," which I did, unsuccessfully and in great shame for the following year; Cash App requests of $150.00 from my little brother and $600.00 from my sister, one with the little emoji symbolizing children's clothes, the other, a bottle; more salacious swimsuit poses from Tierra saying what about this one?; another yo is you ballin Sunday? from Cee, and one you down to hunt tonight? from Wais and B, but not Ray. I mostly think *Do these niggas know I'm at work and make $21.75 an hour per diem plus graduate student stipend of $28,000 yearly from the university?* Maybe since me, the VA, and the bank share custody of this house now it must look wild from the outside like when you see black folks on TV but they still be broke. And sure, GodRaptor69 had told his teacher the other day, after I'd dropped him off at school, that he was allergic to white people, yelled it actually, which of course, of course, was because of "my language"; it's not like he said "white bitches," or "snow honkeys" like Chris from *Pym*, he said "white people,"

damn, and I was just on one of their school trips and
these kids was calling everybody all kinds of dickheads,
the four-year-olds and all. Either way, Ray was supposed
to be around here by now, hoagie and chocolate chip
Otis in hand. And I only got time to respond to a few
messages, those that keep me out of jail—letters from
the family court enforcement unit stay in the mail—
and of course a quick double take at the images from
Tierra, but honestly, of all those things I'm most focused
on the hope that Ray ain't misremember the order: buf-
falo turkey hoagie with Cooper sharp cheddar, hot and
sweet peppers, lettuce, tomato, extra mayo, oregano and
a chocolate chip Otis for the postgame snack.

I'd get to Myra's texts soon enough. The last time
I'd seen her was in her room. I was droppin off the kids
and she wanted me to stay for dinner. Always a dinner.
Things had calmed down a bit, since we hadn't been
to court in a couple months; arrangements were, as I
understood them, settled as much as they ever would
be in terms of money and splitting time. I was taking
out a bunch of student loans to pay child support, but
I figured this was better than returning to the cyclical
degradation of family court and mediations where they
simply ask what she wants and order me to do it under
threat of imprisonment. Plus, at least I was still allowed
to see the kids if she was in a good mood or had business to take care of. And it wasn't bad. The food at least.
I used to hate eating anything she cooked but even I

had to admit it had gotten better. She made three steaks and a lobster and crab boil, which, she told me her older kids—whose father shall not be spoken of—really like. Still, I was tryna keep my distance, keep things calm and avoid arguing, so I was saying goodbye to the kids as soon as we got done eating, kissing them on the cheeks and squeezing them. This seemed to surprise her.

"What about dessert?" she asked. "Don't you don't wanna stay and put them to bed?"

IT WAS A LITTLE after eight and they should have been goin down as it was anyway, but before I had the chance to say anything back, she went on, strict. I was already mad that she wanted them to eat dessert after not eating no food, but that was an old argument, a whole other story that I definitely wasn't gonna win so I let it go, or at least I pretended, per the script.

"I'll start their bath and you can wash them up," she said.

This took too long. It felt like all I could do was hesitate with her. No answer would ever be the right answer. Trying to avoid saying no, which would lead to an argument where I'd become the defendant again, had become unbearable. Unforgettable: infinitely garnished wages, my license suspended, lost jobs, another eviction, even getting kicked out of grad school and never seeing the kids again to top it off; to soothe myself I'd recall my own stupidity in this equation: fucking without a condom or vasectomy in the first place, coming back into the house, ignoring every warning known to the human race for the sole purpose of quelling a mutual loneliness brought on by conditions entirely out of our control. She could always afford a lawyer and I couldn't; she knew the things to say, the pictures to show in court and at what time to describe the many ways, apparently, I'd abused or neglected the children, how to be light-skinned and class savvy and feminine enough to pass for innocent in such matters. She held the records, had the time. And the real terror was that she could be just as cruel as she could be 'loving, even if this was a love drenched in unbearable fantasies, turning always to money as an inverse, the thousands of dollars a month could be twice that when calculating earning potential in the state of Pennsylvania, as I was warned often by her, the lawyers, the judge; earning the PhD would count against me, let alone having to explain the new letters arriving at the university, HR prodding for explanations on why I'd consistently refused to care for my children. Embarrassing. And yet, I knew if I said no, she would start yelling, or grab me, hit me in the chest. I knew that I could, if I wanted to and had the heart, push her off me and roll the fuck out anyway. And I also knew that neither my pockets nor my heart could deal with the consequences.

Over the years though, I had got suspicious of my own acquiescence as she yelled first that I needed to be more vulnerable and then that I was not a victim in an interminable loop of demands for transparency and reality shaming. She laughed and said I was being crazy and I yelled, after the most direct and unsubtle refusal to allow me to see the children, outside of her house— of course, of course, in front of too many neighbors— that she should go to *fucking* therapy, not just regular therapy, in the whisper that proper home training would have otherwise taught me to perform, but yelled *fucking* therapy, like I ain't know better, like that would help the situation in any conceivable way; only later, after I'd filed for joint custody, did I discover that I was being recorded. And I wondered too often if it were better to just say fuck it, to let it all go. Let the chips fall where they might or whatever and tell the kids, when they turned eighteen if I were to be able to find them, everything that had happened between their mom and me. That I tried. Admit defeat to my homies in the black dad group chat all mostly feeling the same, whether lying or telling the truth about what we'd done to get here: my pursuit of out-of-state education over being a "real" and penniless family, Cee's general nonchalance, D's obsessive cheating, J's softness bordering on constant surrender. I could keep all the receipts I had and just let them make a fact-based determination. The future was obvious from the past: the fact that I didn't want her to go to term, versus her excitement at carrying two lives instead of one; when she asked, I should have lied, could have said I too was excited, but instead, the clarity of my nondesire for this only reaffirmed her own; some appointments were canceled, and others were made. And in that final moment, sitting there at the kitchen table before putting the babies in the bathtub, I could have left. But I took the coward's route. I sat my ass down at that kitchen table, ate the chocolate brownie with whipped cream behind which there was the most intense scowl on the planet, and squeezed out a smile from the bottom of my rib cage when I watched the kids gobble it down all messy. Then I took a deep breath and followed her upstairs to bathe them.

The worst part, perhaps, is how badly I still wanted her then, or some version of her where we both got what we needed. I watched her move in that black dress the same way I watched her the first time she cuffed me to her old bed frame back home before climbin on top of me so slow, so gently, so warm, I knew I ain't deserve nothin like it. The way she slid her palms across my chest and cried for me not to cum yet, the way she never wanted to use a condom.

"My bed too," she went on, turning to look at me comin up the steps behind her. "It's bent and saggin. Can you try to fix it while you're here?"

It was a stupid request because we both knew I wasn't never no handyman. But I was dumb. Washing up the kids always made me laugh. Bubble bath or not there's always somethin funny about these two little naked creatures pretending to be fish or making aqua jet noises as they squirt each other with the purple octopus bath toy and giggle and cry and yell and splash and say, "Diddddyyyy!" like I'm the rapper, one pointin at the other to blame him for some slight or another like I'm not sittin right next to them watching the whole thing in real time.

"Come on man, can you stand up?" I said. "Gotta wash that booty."

They both repeated me. They always repeat, dragging out different words each time. "Wash booooty?"

"Yeah boy, wash that booty."

They were dancing, covered in soap and yelling, "Wash that booty! Wash that booty!"

Myra had gone into her room, and as each one finished with booty washing, I dried him off, slapped him on the butt and sent him in there to be clothed and put to bed. I stayed in the bathroom for a while, trying to imagine a way out. I was tryna gather an excuse to leave that even she would have to abide by, something real drastic that she would take seriously, when I was struck by the obvious notion that in this context family is the only seriousness lying underneath the more comical fantasy like those *Fast and the Furious* movies; wasn't there anybody locked up and in need of bail when you need them? Where in the world were the family emergencies now? Maybe, I thought, if I stayed in the bathroom long enough I would gather nerve; the strength might really hit me to just say no, no matter what. And I decided I didn't wanna feel like that anymore. I didn't wanna feel touched that way, I didn't wanna feel convinced. I didn't wanna do whatever she said I had to do. And so I walked out with that kind of determination in mind, and heard her calling.

"Can you come look at this bed please?"

She was still wearing the black dress but had removed her bra and panties using that bed line—seriously, a penny for every time some woman wanted "help" fixin they little-ass too-low-to-the-ground twin bed and perhaps that would be enough money—it was hard to tell whether excitement or resentment would win out in my urge to leave or obey.

"I gotta go," I said. "A lot of work and stuff."

"Really?" she said. "You always say you have to work. Nobody has to work that much. So you're just going to leave just like that right after the kids went to sleep?" She was irritated.

"Yeah, I'm just real tired too."

"Which one is it? Are you tired or you gotta do work? It's not even that late, why are you rushing to leave so much?"

She was getting louder, and I could feel my body

acquiescing, the insecurities about havin sex without a condom, or the fact that it felt, often times when we did fuck, like I had no other choice and it became hard for me to enjoy it because I was too in my head about consequence and continuation. What I did point out though, what I could give in to, as soon as she grabbed my hand, was a certain clarity of desire. No sooner did she pull me toward the bed and place my other hand on her chest did I palm her ass and she rolled on top of me. What was left of the bed frame collapsed, so we laid there lopsided while she dug my dick out and rubbed it against herself, wet already, as if I'd been eating her out, which she actually hadn't let me do in years. And then I thought about how my desire to do so had caused so much conflict because she said it was too intimate when she came like that and I was mad and thinking about how she always claimed I wasn't being intimate enough, and never for a second did I divulge the truth in not trusting her. Ray and Lise agree on this one point that things are simple: that I'm dumb, shoulda just used a condom, so we never really talk about it as the contentions within their own experiences might ring too true.

I reached for a condom and she pushed my hand down, which made me grow harder. It had become a problem lately, sometimes having sex at all, or otherwise maintaining an erection during the preamble and the play, enjoying it just enough to stay hard but not cum right away, and to provide some manner of anal or vaginal penetration for straight women, to play with femme men, or otherwise substitute the reality effect of a cartoonishly hard cock with a worn-out mouth and tongue for anyone else. For the past couple years I'd mostly just been eating pussy till the lover I was with came and then lying and saying I came too and drinking and acting like everything was okay and when the lover would discover that I was lying they would say they wanted me to cum and I would lay there flaccid and feeling good and saying I was feeling good but they rarely believed me and so lovers rarely lasted. There were few exceptions in between, my desperation for Alicia standing out as the prime exception to the rule.

So then Myra was ridin me but I wasn't really thinking about it and even though it felt good I was getting soft. And if I got soft with her on top me of me, and she found out, I would get cussed out and have to fight, so I thought turning more aggressive for a bit might help; I turned her around to fuck her from behind and still, even squeezing her thighs and hearing her beg I was getting soft, panicking. I leaned into it though, squeezing her tighter and pushing and moaning like I was cumming even though she said I better not so soon. She was mad at this, but not as mad as she woulda been if she found out that on her lopsided bed, and in that dress, and inside her, I couldn't stay hard. Unable to go back on what I'd just done either, I ran out to the bathroom to pee. Sitting on the toilet I kept breathing in deep, thinking of a plan to leave. When I came back into the room I told her that I really needed to go, she looked at me like I was crazy and asked if I was for real.

"At least finger me," she said, and grabbed my left hand and put it inside her as I tried to pull away but never using all my strength or looking her in the face, and so I moved my upper body over her head and just closed my eyes to wait until she came, so I could leave. And left too soon nonetheless at this point where it really started; that night into the next morning I tried to describe why I didn't like it, how I did not want to touch or be touched by her anymore, which sparked then the hundreds of formal emails describing her fear of me, my abuse, my endless panic and questions about what this meant before turning solely to acquiescence. Eventually she said, off the record, "I just don't like when you tell me no."

—

"YOU WORRIED YA GIRL ain't gonna wake up?" Lise says. "Hello! Joseph!"

"Annoyed about people messaging me all this dumb shit," I say. "You hungry?"

"Always hungry, but not like we bout to get a break no time soon, why?" Lise wipes under Ms. Johnson's eyes, around her face. "And you know damn well you gotta ignore that shit. It's what you get for bein a little slut anyway. Gettin slutted out, Ms. Johnson and everybody else done had a piece."

I stare at her for a second. She's flipping her braids outta the way with her shoulder and elbow. There's purple in them now and it looks nice. "Shut the fuck up," I say. "I was offering you food cause my friend sposed to drop some off, miss two different shiftless niggas cummin in her for like four years talkin bout you in love with this little beady-eyed Furby downstairs."

She laughs. "Look man, I definitely made some mistakes. I swore this nigga was fly cause he rode a bicycle and recycled. I can't believe I let this nigga cum in me it's so embarrasing. I can't believe this shit sometimes. Fucking crazy," she says. I laughed at the way she told this story, a glimpse into a past self that I never knew, and could probably never fully know. "Yeah that shit be fun when it's happenin, but damn. The shit I used to do for this nigga." She tidies up Ms. Johnson a little more. "And what friend, Ray, the cute one? He a baddie but just so fucking annoying," she says. "Tell him just get me whatever you get."

People been calling Ms. Johnson my girl because of a combinatory assumption that I'm some kind of cougar hunter on one end—based on workplace rumor (which always contains some truth)—and on the other, the plain fact that Ms. Johnson, when awake, always says the nastiest shit to me and asks whenever possible that I be the one to attend to her. This was normal, in part, from all the time working private ambulance companies for the Northeast Philly Russians, in and out of those nursing homes that might as well have been Temple's campus where sexual activity was concerned, except these were too-old-to-give-a-fuck old ladies excited to regale me with tales of their fine ass bald-head boyfriends down the hall while I'm taking them to and from dialysis all the way in South Philly. It's to the point that whenever Ms. Johnson comes in and I'm not at work people just text me like ya girl here looking for you, or you better come service this woman nigga! Once, she had a UTI and just kept screaming all through the morning the evening and the night, "Where is Joseph! Joseph! Joseph! Joseph! Where is Joseph! Joseph! Joseph! Oh lordie help me! Where is Joseph! Joseph! Joseph!" and it was both deeply sad and strange and unbearably common and the laughter was unprecedented, and I would like to say the sadness was too, but it was not.

"And don't worry about Ms. Johnson," I say. "She obviously bout to outlive you, all that peach-flavored Moscato and shit."

"Imma be in jail anyway, wine be damned, if Isiah say one more word to me today."

IN THE AFTERMATH OF washing ass I return to the ED. A boy who used to beat me up is here for STD testing.

I refresh the screen over and over, fiending for results. There's a couple in the hall outside room 14; their son is getting stitches and they arguing—first about whose fault it is that he jumped from the couch through the glass table, then about who gave who the herpes. I recall The Long One jumping from the couch and through the glass table and asking, as she laughed and laughed until she didn't, why she thought it was so funny, my chest tight as hell. There's this one ED regular, a man my age having a sickle cell crisis on a hallway bed. He gives me the nigga nod as we make eye contact. He always does that. In the room next to him are two young bouls from Central, athletes eating chicken and broccoli with extra gravy. I can tell by the scent, the slightly lighter tone of the rice and thinness of the gravy that it's from Crystal Garden around the corner, that place where even after I'd found the maggot in my shrimp with lobster sauce that time I kept eating at until they closed down. One of the boys is wearing those red-and-white comfy Nike socks that Foot Locker used to sell for $13.00 which are now $30.00, and the other is lying on the stretcher in shorts and a T-shirt.

"Ayo old head," they yell. "Can I get some water, man?" And I give them some ice water and apple juice.

In the trauma bay there's a lanky girl I knew from middle school named Diamond. She's the first woman I met in real life and regarded as unquestionably beautiful, funny, a genius; she is even kind, which I assumed back then, given history, was simply a trick, a half-school-year-long plot to embarrass me in public later on. Lauryn Hill and Brandy, Monica and Aaliyah, Jennifer Lopez and Toni Braxton, Christina Aguilera and Gwen Stefani, T-Boz, Left Eye and especially Chili were, yes, boyhood crushes, but Diamond was the girl of what I might have been too ashamed to call my dreams. She stood almost as tall as me and almost as awkward when we were kids. The first thing I did when we got dial-up internet was look up how old you had to be to get emancipated and marry someone, specifically Diamond. After which I tried to earn said emancipation money playing online Texas Hold Em on my grandfather's computer as he lay rotting on the sunken mattress next to his rum-filled mini fridge. Diamond ain't know about none of this. At school I was still pissing and shitting myself and getting smacked around by kids half my size with twice the confidence and much less of a future to consider, confused about how she may or may not have been in on it.

When I walk into the bay, I don't think she'll recognize me.

"Hey Joseph," she says. "How have you been? I ain't know you worked here."

"I don't," I say. "Just hangin around like everybody else."

She chuckles. I begin asking her what happened and what's going on, but maybe it's obvious. She has cuts

on her face. Her hair is disheveled. And she's very pregnant; "She might pop at any moment," the nurse says.
Her uncle sits next to her in a folding chair, smiling
slightly. He looks tired the way all men of his station do.

I don't look at her chart, since I feel like it would
be an invasion of her privacy, but she says it was a car
accident. There's a feeling of stupidity washing over me
as I realize it wasn't the other thing, but I woulda felt
stupid for not thinkin that other thing just the same. I
don't wanna talk to her because she already used the
phrase *How have you been?* An indicator that I've learned
to read as *I don't wanna fucking talk to you but I'll be polite*,
her body canted in a way that suggests discomfort in the
conversation, or maybe she's just in pain. Nothin broken
though; the baby is fine, fake smiles all around. She's
been completely worked up already which gives me the
urge to leave, knowing that beyond the most basic forms
of prep and stabilization, activities of daily living, I am
ultimately useless. She looks me up and down too slowly,
and with her big ass eyes I don't think she's tryna hide it.
Her uncle relaxes into a frown, one of those dark brown
and handsome old heads, dignified in how his own
salt-and-pepper chivalry hasn't collapsed into the era of
twerking and text messaging, the folds of his face held
up stern by the technophobic superiority of his moral
resolve, which essentially means he's been cheating on
her aunt for forty years and everyone has come to accept
it as a lesser evil within the patriarchal world system on

account of his good union job with the city; it's always "with the city," like this nigga could be Ya Fave Trashman or be on Peco or PGW time, it's all pretty much the same. His hat, however, is hideous. Diamond has incredible dimples: Are her teeth still a little jagged, like a lanky baby alligator? There's a tiny bit of space between each one, but not enough to be called a gap, and she doesn't smile like other people do, with their teeth or gums, that annoying, privileged smile of folks who always felt good doing so. My first kiss was with her at one of those traveling carnivals, having stopped at Wyoming instead of Whitehall now because of all the shooting at our middle school, and maybe if I remember right we were in some kind of ball pit and it was dark enough for us both to smile simultaneously and I wanted to kiss her dimples then, so I had my mouth semiclosed and leaning toward a cheek but she went full open mouth and the initial exchange was messy; maybe I should've said something about how I adored her cheeks and things would have been different.

"What?" she says.

"Nothin," I say. "I just didn't think I was gonna randomly see you at my job like twenty years later."

Her nurse comes up to me from behind, and before I can turn around she puts one hand on my waist, her ring and pinky fingers wrapped around and sliding down the top of my iliac crest, pushing the Savage Fenty draws just low enough for the embrace of skin and its cold, her ring also soothing. "Joseph," she says, "can you take her to L&D for me babe, she's already been cleared here."

While I both love and hate it, I don't bother addressing the fact that she always calls me babe, baring her skin along that part of my body I always wanted to look like D'Angelo's near nether regions in the "How Does It Feel" music video because all the girls I knew loved it so much. Either way I want her to touch me more and less but then she turns and goes back to her work computer, the infinite inputs of quality control having long since taken precedent over patient care.

Diamond says, "So Joseph, you gonna take me to L&D?"

Pushing her rickety wheelchair with one arm down the hall I can't help but say "skrt skrt" at every adjustment, hitting sharp turns around people who decide not to move, we skrt around a little boy in respiratory distress, skrt past a drunk man who calls me a "bitch ass faggot nigga anyway" cause I wouldn't get him a apple juice as I slide an open code cart out of our way with one hand, skrting with the other, used EKG pads stuck to the outside and empty vials scattered on top of it and feeling surrounded by everything that didn't save a life.

"How you been?" I say.

Diamond says, "I think you can figure this one out." She looks up at me, her face just inches from mine, noses near touching, and we both laugh. Her one arm flails out of the wheelchair and she shakes it, adding to the drama of failed equipment, clowning the whole thing.

"It was all I could find," I say, laughing. Skrt, skrt. I ask her if it's her first kid. Not like I really want to ask this, or to know, though I kind of already know.

"No," she says. "I got older ones at home, and what about you?"

My son, who was born while I was in Iraq after his mom stopped taking birth control because I was leaving but didn't say so, is texting me about dinner; he'd like to cook something from the *Food Wars* cookbook I'd got him last Christmas and I'm like why not. The Long One wants to ride bikes to her girlfriend house down the street and the two little ones want to do whatever the old ones are doing but are nowhere near prepared: "Can I help cooking!?" "I wanna ride bikes too!" is all I can hear now and the negotiation of generational difference between the siblings erupting into physical violence and crying. What I say to Diamond is that I have four little fuckers at home. What I don't say is that after coming home from said Baghdad workcation I blew a bunch of my money on a nice apartment that I never left and did nothing but drink and fuck people I hated for months until trying to kill myself with pills from the VA, *like a teenage girl,* my then lover who should not have been my lover says, "Like a made-for-TV PTSD movie," I think. I do not tell her that my then lover, who was living with her boyfriend, had a daughter, that I will find out that she is my daughter. I do not tell her or anyone things that will make us uncomfortable or laugh in the wrong way or at the wrong things. I do a cost-benefit analysis in my head of being a consistent nigga number three on one's platter, the gains and losses, triumphs and availability, or the exhaustion and conforming and property relations and mascing up and picket-fence pretense required to be someone's number one dick delivery person.

"Are you still with the mom?" she asks. She knows damn well I'm not but wants to hear me say it.

"No," I say. "And what about you?" I want to imagine that she asks because she's interested. That there's something to save, that there will be some saving.

"No," she says. "My boyfriend is at home now, different dads." There's a loneliness I can't name, or that I can name but only to myself, which makes me want to be alone even more. We start to tire of the conversation, the repetition. The lack of a plan, yet predictability of a future. Diamond's car accident is a minor scrape and even though her whole hoopdie is totaled, it's just another expected hurdle. Considering the horrors that would have ensued had we ever gotten together, it only makes sense that I'd assumed she was beaten, rather than having wrecked her car, some things feeling more eternally likely on this side of the world.

I swipe my ID badge to open the sliding glass doors

into Labor and Delivery. A new nurse checks Diamond in and I help her get into bed.

"Thank you Joseph," she says.

"See you later," I say. "Any time, good luck!" And is this shame I feel reverting to default forms of communication?

After dropping her off I check my computer screen incessantly, refreshing again and again over the boy's name I knew from elementary school. He's still waiting. Our exchanges terminated back in the day after I'd discovered the power of accessing another's discomfort, transforming his marks of my being a sissy and my mom a crackhead and my grandfather a sissy I started going in on his reading skills. Not for nothin, but this was after I'd been jumped by him and a few other niggas on several accounts resulting in stitches twice and a broken arm once; this is not an excuse for my behavior, but I think valuable context for what I'm about to reiterate about another human being's mental capacity; he appeared to be shocked at the simplicity of my claims that he was, despite everything, a retard—yes, it was in that era, and how I despise when people revise the things they actually said or did in the name of individual progress—who was destined for lifelong sadness and impoverishment just like his ugly ass illiterate daddy with the peezy patchy beard, how he should be embarrassed for not knowing how to say words like "rigorous" and that more importantly, when he died, no one would either care or remember him; in fact, more folks would celebrate, whenever the event happened, hopefully soon, even in the unlikely scenario that with his limited capacity for thinking he lived past high school and forced some woman to love and have children with him, they too would patiently wait for the moment he died, so that they could be free of his absolute stupidity and uselessness. I'm paraphrasing. He responded, quietly, that I was being weird, but he never bothered me much again.

When I finally check my phone I see all these missed calls from Ray, who never really calls, only texts. There are voice mails and voice messages, the latter of which I continue to wish never existed. I'd check into them but Black Top is in the room behind me and needs his dressings changed; when I enter, he just shakes his head.

"Worth it this time?" I ask.

"Man," he says. "Fuck is worth?"

Black Top been at Holmesburg a hot minute. Not his first time. The first time he'd almost killed this nigga with brass knuckles for stalking his aunt and, unable to afford bail, he started signing up for the trials at the urging of Red Top who'd told him it was all good. The soft-core stuff wasn't paying enough though and so he'd escalate, not all the way to LSD trials by the army in the trailers out back, but mid-tier activities a bit more upscale than skin or shampoo sampling. In the office right next to an industrial sink the medical techs pulled his fingernails off with pliers to measure rates of regrowth after the application of some gel designed to stimulate the body's own efforts, which we both joked would turn him into a lizard and which he agreed might result in better treatment. We are both, him and I, under the impression that he's getting nothing but the placebo cream on this one given how long it takes for them to grow back each time. He got used to it though, as one adjusts to anything unfortunate if forced to live in it long enough, and even after he'd been out a few years, he figured why not return to what he knew next time he got locked up. This time he'd killed one of his children after his wife left. Not on purpose though. On occasion he'd drift into talking about his child before trailing off into what he would do once he proved his case and got out. In the hospital he watches reality TV and asks me not to "click the little boxes" that inform the docs I already changed his dressings so he might stay longer. Regarding my father, Black Top most often refers to him as sniveling, and recounts the times the other man tried to proposition him.

"Rell," he says. "This nigga baby food. Soft."

Not like I was asking but this is the kind of comparative analysis Black Top often volunteers. "Ion't know why you askin after that nigga anyway."

No one does, really. The pursuit is too often baffling, despite making perfect sense. It was Black Top who figured I was Rell's son in the first place. "Them ears," he recognized from the first time I walked into his room. He'd regale me with tales of my father's punk ass-ness and how a man like him could end up in Holmes-burg in the first place. Deeply bored by the classical trajectory of the birth-to-prison pipeline, I'd often dig details out of him instead. Turns out, Rell loves matcha tea, fat women, and *Law & Order: SVU*. Apparently this nigga crochets. This is a fact that Black Top returns to often, confused by the gesture altogether, and wonder-ing whatever happened to sewing, the old Royal Dansk cookie tin one's grandmother might keep stashed on top of the frigerator with the real equipment in it. This, for Black Top, is the greatest sign that we're losing anything right or pure in the culture. Enjoying his fully gray hair, pure white almost, he asks how I'm losing mine at damn near half his age and I tell him that it's because he is stressing me out, to which he says I should stop being a bitch and reminds me that he had his first stroke at twenty-nine.

He wants to know if I got a girl or a wife or a little boyfriend. What I don't say is anything about love, what feels like its lack of possibility whether from individual dysfunction on account of being a male as per the for-mula, or the innumerable social, financial, historical or familial barriers making it hardly possible on top of the fact that perhaps I'm coming to like myself a little too much to delimit minuscule free time to the context of serving and being of service. Sometimes, in the deep

dark nightmares conjured by antidepressants or melatonin, I'm in my house cleaning up after another grown
person's clothes and dishes again, listening to how men
ain't shit, wasn't never shit, and ain't never gonna be shit
under the not-so-subtle suggestion that I work less and
spend more time on costly outings or casual cuddling,
and fixing light bulbs and smashing spiders, arguing
about the proper form of discipline for the children
who no one else will treat like actual people, and within
this oblivion, screamed at by upper-middle-class persons working an eighth of the time while lying in bed,
I'm offered everything that might help make a better
life possible except, of course, help. Just vibe-oriented
conditions of possibility. Though I'm learning, however
slowly, or too fast, depending on who you ask, the more
appropriate role of confession, to admit more openly
and more often that these things are conditionally my
fault, to quit making everything so complicated, apologize, and seek redemption in the classroom, on the
internet, in the bowels of the home or bottom of the
river, through careful, devoted, and unceasing attention
to others' needs. Some version of this slips from thought
to lips and Black Top says I'm just being a bitch again
and need to find a wife. Since this seems to have turned
out so well for him, and because a room just freed up
next door after a patient went AWOL, I let it ride and
plan on returning later.

    While I'm cleaning off the empty stretcher, Beens,

my favorite person in housekeeping who had a heart attack a few weeks ago, thanks me for the due diligence. We get to talking and he's telling me about these Afro-centric soaps he makes, how he got more in stock now even the bergamot or whatever one I'd been buying out all the time and I'm racked with infinitesimal pleasure at the prospect of soothing my body with this soap. Beens is also telling me about his son, the one who, even after getting him a job at our hospital, kept popping up high or coming in late or calling out or cussing out the manager and now don't got nothing near stable work with a baby on the way and how he wishes that, like me, instead of cheating on his pregnant girlfriend, his son would get his head on straight. This makes me wonder if I'm projecting a radically different vision of my life and history or if the bar has sunk beneath the floor and if just getting married and binge cheating like everyone else would make me happy. Beens never forgets to remind me that he's proud, and that my mom and them must be proud, no matter how often I ain't proud of pretty much anything except the fact that I can clean some shit.

I leave Beens in the room cleaning cause there's a code in room 12 and thankfully, Rasheeda is already over there doing CPR, so rather than all the minutiae I'm just relieving her tense ass triceps after cracking through all the patient's ribs. This patient feels mushy to be honest, and when I actually look up at his face it's pretty clear he's gone. The familiarity in him is frustrating though, seeing black folks who look like my folks die by the thousands while I'm touching them is a particular kind of horror. I feel light and heavy and hungry and tired at once. The man feels flat and dead. By the time they call it, my stomach is growling so obviously that Louie notices, his notepad in one hand, smacking me on the ass with the other and saying, "Little hungry there, big guy?"

I step back from the dead man, drop my gloves in the trash can and sanitize my fingers before snatching the whole pack of Twizzlers out of Louie's scrub pocket. He's charge nurse today, and we're short, so he's too busy to try and catch up with me as I speed-walk into an empty room and Rasheeda follows behind to grab some.

"They knew damn well this nigga was gone when they rolled him in here," she says, scarfing down the Twizzlers. "Like yall really tryna get me buff out here." She grabs a few more.

"But you are buff," I say, squeezing her muscle as she flexes.

"Buff enough for this break. Imma go to the back real quick, so can you help restock 12 and watch trauma for me? You know Isiah dumb ass not doing shit."

"I got you," I say. "I'm hungry as shit though, what you got?"

"Johnny made goulash last night," she says. "You can have some later but don't be out here tellin everybody it's in there."

"Word."

Rasheeda is the kind of black woman who know lots of things and people and is too tired to bother saying much about it; she's at least part of the reason I got this job, as her husband been cuttin my hair since I had any, but she's also one of those personal trainers who takes clients up to the art museum steps before sunrise and never eats out. Since hers is the longest relationship I've known between two black people I often ask her how, and her response is always some version of the fact that I don't have any patience. When I tell her I don't have any time she just says some version of yes, that is true, but what I do have is choices. I grab a big white body bag from the closet and head back over to 12 so we can wrap the body up, fumbling with the little strings on the toe tags, and Louie is looking at me like *Did this nigga really eat all the Twizzlers that fast?* And I'm looking at him like *Is you gonna help?* And his ass over there flirting with one of the cops again, this big bald dude who done ran through half the ED and who Lise took to calling Low Fat Deebo. Low Fat Deebo used to be married to this little white nurse but she was stealing Percs and pissed hot and got fired, so now maybe she's in rehab or on the street in Kensington. When I finally finish unfurling the complicated-for-no-reason strings on the toe tags I get the first one on and then I look over at Louie, hoping he'll help me roll the body before all the shit comes out and he still running his mouth, but rolls his eyes and relents.

"You are such a fuckin hater," he says.

"Yeah I hate what yall doin to my back," I say.

"Don't let management hear that," Louie says, tossing his clipboard on the code cart.

I bend my legs as much as I can before turning the body so Louie can slide the bag underneath, during which he's struck by an idea, some hazy memory of the future, and he's like, "Oh yeah! You comin to my cookout this Sunday? It's gonna be some cuties there too, I promise."

I take a deep breath and pull and lift toward my body, the ET tube drooling across the bare skin on my arm reminding me I shoulda wore a gown but all I could think about was food. I'd forgotten all about this cookout even though I had planned on going at first and just bringing the kids with me cause it's so close. It's always a ton of people there anyway, including kids since Louie live in that part of the Northeast where my mixed cousins and all the Ricans who say nigga live; the average person over there got 3.5 kids.

"Nah I can't imma be out of town," I say.

He's shocked, sarcastically. "Nooo, where you goin?"

I consider saying something about visiting his mother back home, his mother who is so fine she caused a minor labor strike when she came to see him at work one time and men, women and children was like *That's Louie mom? Get the hell outta here, his little goofy ass? Who the daddy?* But instead I tell him about Belize and he smiles. "Uh-huh...Tierra said she was going there too."

I don't say anything else but finish zipping up the body and raising the stretcher a little higher to go downstairs. When I pull off Louie grabs the clipboard and says, "Good luck!" and strolls away laughing. My stomach growls again, with more of a pang this time, so I reach over Kristen sitting at the nurses' station and grab a few almond Hershey's Kisses and, as she mean mugs me, I pop them in my mouth and put my gloves on to head down with the body.

EVERY ONCE IN A while, I'll look up patient information that I have no work-related reason to look up. I'm a very curious individual, I guess, and so this time I want to know a bit about the body from room 12 but he's still listed as a John Doe with little else other than the assumptions regarding a long history of isms, medical problems and extreme lack of resources or people willing and able to provide them. In the basement, we're alone and I talk to him a little. I ask what he liked to do in his spare time and if dying was part of that plan. I often wonder, when I see other dead black men, how lonely they were, and if they too ever wanted to die but lacked the courage or follow-through. These are the kinds of questions too boring to ask the living, too boring now even for my therapist, or friends or lovers, too boring for my mother, brother or sister. Maybe only the dogs are attuned to it. I ring the bell on the morgue door, which always strikes me as unusually pleasant, this kind of high-pitched ring like a made-for-TV suburban family's house, and just as empty. When no one comes I just slide all the other bodies to the side, maybe thirteen of them, and shove the new one in as best I can. If no one comes to empty it out soon we'll have nowhere to put them, they'll have nowhere to be.

I'm almost sneaking back upstairs because honestly I wanna make it from the stairwell door to the break room without anyone seeing me so I can finally get some damn food and see what Ray supposed to be doing with my hoagie from Lee's. In the hall I try and call him back but he doesn't answer. In a fit of desperation I dash into the break room and eat a couple spoons of Rasheeda's goulash that Johnny—a mid-tier cook at best—made last night and, unlike the center, it'll have to hold. Susan pops out of her office and starts tryna chat me up but I'd really rather not; she's always clocking everybody's time and goes back to check the computer for when people come in and out, how long folks' lunch breaks are etc. etc. A whack middle managerial tactic that could be made more interesting if she had a sense of humor or wasn't racist but one thing I will say about

Susan is that she's not afraid, like many of the other snow honkeys working here, and she says the most outrageous Judge Judy–type shit to noncompliant patients that linger somewhere between entirely too fucked up and early 2000s *Chappelle's Show* skit which, depending on who you ask, might be the same thing. She thinks we're cool though because I do my job and mind my business, which in this case means saying nothing about her and D fucking in that break room decontamination stall nobody uses, so she keeps tryna recruit me as a pal, and since I don't feel like dealing with her I just wave politely before walking out of the break room under the pretense that I would never take an unauthorized break and was, in fact, exercising my sensitivity to the environment by grabbing a breather upon the death of yet another child, of which there are many, and of which this is an acceptable reason to take a breather, like nicotine addiction, in the way that few other things are.

I position myself at a standing computer so as to avoid sleep and log back into the system. It's not altogether clear to me why the ED is the best place for writing, but certainly I owe my writing life's existence and this text in its current formation to the fact that Google Docs isn't a blocked site at the hospital. The waiting room is full. Among my tasks, official and not, is to keep an eye on the waiting room and drag patients back who've been assigned a slot in the next line of waiting— or hallway beds more likely—for inspection until we say it's okay for them to leave, to anticipate their needs and the needs of nurses and providers and other techs; anyone coming in for STD testing obviously needs a urine sample, anybody with chest pain over 40 needs an EKG, mental health patients need a 1:1, and anybody in labor or bleeding and screaming or shot or in shock or unconscious is high priority for a bed and a provider's attention. There are, of course, exceptions.

I open another tab to a folder titled "Dissertation," which has all the readings I tend to forget a few minutes after reading them despite a twinge of excitement at certain turns of phrase or deployments of narrative or syntactical treachery. There are thirteen different files which say chapter 1, some of them repeats and others novels, memoirs, critical testimonies; despite my disinterest in chapters altogether, my agent says this will make selling the work easier, the chapters, having a clear narrative arc and interest in satisfying the reader's desire for cathexis (or was it catharsis?), self-improvement, transparency, and cleanness. While I don't think such a thing could be called realism, I do need money and attempt to negotiate these gross assaults on mental activity as best I can. I am penning a kaleidoscopic private plane ride through the psyches of men like my father, and grandfather too, who were both experimented on at Holmesburg, the most profitable prison still standing today, snatching up swaths of real estate along Tacony and State Road and making home feel like home. I've got *Acres of Skin* and *Survival Math* and *Soul on Ice* and the like propped up at my at-work writing desk. The dissertation and the writing being two separate yet unequal species, the latter more than the former will, in standard lukewarm left-of-center liberal fashion, unveil all manner of isms and subjections through which we have survived and continue to live pointing toward the reiteration of formal uplift mechanisms which no one will admit have failed and, ultimately, be read by not a single person I love. It will be historical. It will be sociological. It will be powerful, I guess. The former is for my niggas and them who I hope to get into reading books as well as they more reactively read people. Lise fucks with it and Ray thinks I should stop being a coward and use his real name. One holds the promise of sliding out of poverty for the long haul with time to love my children and the other is forcing the growth of a too-small-for-too-long heart. I can't focus though because I'm near hallucinating about this hoagie and Otis that I as of yet do not have, much like any more patience or brain power given the limited amount of proteins and carbohydrates my body has available in the present moment. Just as I'm being nosey looking at people's charts when I should be working on the writing, I start hallucinating about the Otis, that sweet, sweet Otis Spunkmeyer muffin that I will lay promptly in the freezer for a spell before biting into it so slowly, the muffin's chill will sink into my teeth as I do into its thick and tender chocolaty core.

A trauma comes in. Stumbling through the automatic ED doors like the drunks do but not drunk because he's holding his face and quite bloodied in a designer white T; the cut is something immaculate between runway model and Technicolor cartoon superhero. From where I stand behind another set of doors he's quite tall and muscular, though hunched over, and elicits gasps from the right triage nurse, Amy, who's habitually unbothered, so much so that she once told this dude missing half his hand from one of those illegal contracting gigs outside of Home Depot he'd have to wait to be called, sat his ass down and handed him a towel, mopping up the blood on the floor before opening a pack of Gushers—though this time she jumps up in true snow bunny fashion (her own words of self-reference) and yells for help, yells that someone needs to get a stretcher now, and pushes malingerers out of the way. Louie notices and darts over; even Isiah appears outta nowhere donning gloves and a gown, all tiny and eager. Feeling obligated to help, I finish this sentence before putting my gloves on. Everyone swarms the patient and with no available stretchers they hobble into the bay holding tight under the trauma's arms.

ME AND RAY FIRST met on the bus to Iraq. It was technically the bus to Milwaukee where we would train for the never-ending desert war but we called it the bus to Iraq anyway because that's how it felt. We were both unknowingly sleeping with this woman named Jacqui from Nicetown which, upon discovery—"Oh you know Jacqui too?"—he thought was scary and I thought was funny and she thought was funny, though her now ex-husband did not think was funny as he spammed us both on Facebook Messenger asking for details about "what we did" as if we'd pledged allegiance to this nigga at some altar. Jacqui said he had a bunch of girlfriends anyway and we'd all laugh later playing *Borderlands* together with Jacqui and her new wife while me and Ray sat next to each other in our shipping container room with one cut-out window. Ray and I, two of the eleven blacks in the unit we deployed with which included folks from PA, Milwaukee, Puerto Rico, and an Air Assault unit from Georgia, would be roommates for the year and, should I die on any mission as the sole medic, he was set to replace me.

While some of the Rican dudes were with us, others were white. None of the black soldiers really cared to talk about conquering Iraq like that, except this one Nigerian dude who never said "nigga" except when referring to a former president and always with the hard *R*. The symbolic in politics, the racism, the sexism, these things had already bored us for so long, just like the guilt of those newly discovered liberals who just then, six months into a forever war that should have, like most all wars waged by the empire and elsewhere, been illegal—where the legal vs. illegal had already been a bit of a sardonic double bind—come to discover their conscience after one of these psychos mows down a human fleeing in an open field with a vehicle-mounted .50-cal just because he planted a small bomb that didn't even kill anyone. We were willing to participate in this much the same way we were willing to participate in any other job we hated with worse benefits and a higher risk of death or mutilation for ourselves and others back home. Lots of people cried when they took away the .50-cals and replaced them with M249s, arguing that they were more annoying to clean. It was astonishing to see any human being, especially from the United States of America, wake up one day all the way in their twenties and suddenly discover that they might have done something wrong along the way. Maybe. Or just as bad, the pride taken by all manner of snow honkeys and coons and self-assured machismo spokespeople in their patriotism, whose bewildering faith in the U.S.A. could never be made sense of.

Instead, Ray and I mostly spoke about which family members needed money or to be dragged from a crack house and who we might call or email to get it done while we were gone, who had snapped, got shot or stabbed and been lost for good, or the shrinking category of who might still make it. Our bets were never on the parents we were tasked to raise, but on our brightest days we hoped a sibling or two might slip through the cracks; once home these questions would shift into which places we still needed, or felt like we needed, to carry guns to, or who had committed suicide in the few months of our newfound physical health and freedom.

Getting blown up or shot at lost its fervor a few months in; Ray and I shared comparisons to the dangers of growing up which no one else thought were funny. The death rate at Broad and Olney, or up Wiss, or along the Tacony or in Frankford or up North was higher than that of American soldiers in Iraq. We shared shifts in comportment and collective fuck yous not to fear but anticipation; the terror transitioned into jokes and giggles, the once-wacky waving inflatable-arm flailing-tube man of kinetic response transformed into a more attuned *meh* reaction at explosions and transformed into rage or tears as a unit only after actual death was verified.

A most important event returns to me whenever I see Ray though, whenever he offers me one of those nasty ass aloe juices or asks when I'll start working out again. The Avenged Sevenfold concert. A first for us, past a year of our meeting. Our first concert attendance ever, in Baghdad, on Camp Victory, right in front of the PX. This band Avenged Sevenfold tours military bases in occupied territory during active conflict because they love the troops. I'd considered investigating if this also happened in, say, Japan during World War II but decided against it. This happened on my one accidental day off as a medic, as there was red air and too much of a risk to go on a route-clearing mission. This dude Los I used to play ball with had just been killed a week before and like five of us were mad we couldn't get off work to attend the funeral. And so Avenged Sevenfold comes to the PX to entertain us. Though "us" is such a tricky and often wasteful word. When I asked Ray if he wanted to go it took a while for him to let me in. I'd just got done playing ball and was knocking on our locked door while he beat his dick, completely naked with his laptop out, the *Borderlands* load screen on the TV, and Dasha's face on the smaller screen just talking then, perhaps coaching him through it. His dick is big enough that even though his hands are larger than mine, they looked smaller when he stroked it, not quite taking after his favorite actor Wesley Pipes, but a close second. It's sometimes nice and slow, but most times too aggressive, kind of an angsty teen hand job style that looks painful or, forcing the cum to come in that way that, as we age, mandates this kind of vigor and focus for climax on the third or fourth time of any given day. I've judged him both a great deal for leaving the window shade open, his general positioning—both regarding the window and his posture—but most of all for using that mini bottle of cocoa butter lotion like a young boul hiding in his mother's bathroom, rather than investing in some more reasonable lubrication. But every time he reminds me he's saving his money to buy his mom a house. He's sweating, and perhaps in the best shape of our lives; this sometimes makes me jealous, but I could never work as hard on my body as he did, so it never felt unfair. I recognized that he wouldn't get back down to earth until he came, so I just stood there watching, waiting. He always begged and said *I love you* as he came, sometimes with one finger in his ass, other times holding the computer tight up against his body, hugging it to his stomach or propped up on one knee aiming into a brown T-shirt that had gotten too small, which he'd later throw away or give to some little white boy unwashed. When he was done, I unlocked the door and walked in.

"You know," I said, "there's better ways to do this."

He said nothing, and just put his shorts on over the

Spandex drawls like he was getting ready for the gym. "You not goin to the concert?" I asked.

Ray looked at me sideways and said something about me being hype on that whiteboy shit and I had looked at him like he was crazy cause I could always hear Breaking Benjamin through his headphones on my side of the shipping container. Plus, we had already had all those old ass boring conversations about how shitty it was to call black people acting white just because they didn't have big afros or listen exclusively to neo soul, which we both agreed was just R&B anyway. We were supposedly past that. And to be honest, me and Ray bonded over the fact that we both had to deal with that shit too much as kids for not droppin gerunds enough or measuring up to the threat level other people had in mind, particularly the people we wanted to love us, but couldn't, those black people attuned to that other America, who didn't know what crack smelled like and would refuse this knowing at all costs. So I was surprised at his reaction. I just remember him sitting there unfurling the wrapper from that last Otis—a chocolate one we had in our mini fridge that I'd been plottin on all day—and scowling at me like I broke his heart. And maybe I did. I think we were both sad and lonely the whole time we were deployed because even though we had each other, we still didn't really have ourselves.

At the concert I was alone. All the hood niggas I

was fond of stayed back to chat online with their girl-friends at home or suck each other's dicks under slightly delimited conditions of surveillance. I couldn't get into the feeling even though the music was good, which is to say the artistry was there, the kind of per-formance one might read a deft article about after the fact that uses words like "electric" or "melodious," com-paring songs like "Gunslinger" or "Dear God" from the self-titled album I remember Ray and I both listen-ing to on those long nights riding around searching for bombs. Taking a step back and seeing everybody in uniform with rifles, M249s and barettas—the same baretta I accidentally carried into work and left in my locker—jumping up and down and screaming with joy, tan boots crunching into the gravel, it all felt so strange and volatile. What the fuck were we even doing? I left early and came back to an empty room; Ray had gone off somewhere and didn't even bother leaving a note. Excited by the prospect of being alone, I locked the door and closed the shade, placing the computer and hard drive just so between my legs. Though I didn't need to watch anything to cum, say, the first or sec-ond time—pure memory was enough there—it was a luxury to shop around the hard drive, perusing the thousands of shared files in every category imaginable as with great anticipation I untucked my aspiring eight inches of flesh from those too-big camo pants. And in this, both size and selection, I was rather basic by comparison: All the "chicks with dicks" and "blood and scat" and fantasies of people dressed as cats and "interracial" this or "colossal black dick" that or "negro hoes who know" were there—though yes, I had on occasion cum to the film *Sleepwalkers* as a youth—I neither advocated for nor disposed entirely of sexual scripts in the world cage; I had already been begged to do "worse" toward the kind of climax Usher thought he was singing about, and had questions, in fact, about how much of a difference genitalia made in the specific sex act(s) given my narrow experience with other "men" or "women" of differing genital composition; and no, I never had particular beefs one way or the other with people's goofily obsessive interracial shit like Ray who could never stand white girls one bit, who on his mother's life swore that letting one touch you was a high crime of the flesh, nor was I ever kept up at night by the never-ending cavalcade of "important" literature obsessively beholden to mixing or mixedness or people's white wives or husbands, hiding them deep within their subconscious or Instagram stories as it appears in the work; though it is true, it is quite true, that I have never developed a penchant for the warmth of another's non-cum fluids on my flesh or elsewhere, it's all fine where it's all desire, the stronger the better— but by basic I mean whatever happened to some slow sucking and licking of assholes and dicks and pussies and chests and necks and sloppy kissing in between and grasping at each other with palpable need and some penetration maybe at negotiated angles, some standing and sitting and face riding, the starting off slow till you hear the sounds, the never-close-enoughness of bodies succumbed to the depth of each other till there is no choice but to change pace, all liquid now, nowhere else to go but inside another, the sweat and tears, the hands and fingers desperate to live life in the gasps, oh my fucking god, the sounds that release makes, all the melting away, and the confusion about what the hell a world even is in those moments, and sure, I've been called romantic for these gestures while never explicitly precluding my desires from any of the aforementioned, though to put it more simply this is also a problem of language. And I think, remembering now, this is why Louie laughed at Belize, and why Lise asked, "Are you sure?" when Tierra started coming over; maybe they are accounting for the danger of giving this language over too readily, too desperately, to another who knows better than one's self, how to use it.

—

THAT NIGHT OF THE concert was the only night we never spoke about afterward. Innumerable arguments and apologies have come and gone and this stands as the exception. And so when we got home from deployment and began our reacclimation to the old aggressions, when we slipped into previous patterns of necessity and containment, this time getting infinitesimally better at harm reduction, at moving through the rapidly expanding world, there was little to say about ourselves then, and so much to say about everything else. We were in college, we were making art, we were two black boys who made it, or who would make it, given enough head and heart pain. And yet, as big as Ray was on intellectual inquiry and everything, you know, the examined life some call it, he liked to ask big questions and contemplate his own life's relationship to those questions like war, racism, capitalism, sexism, human rights and the prison industrial complex et al. He did not believe my dad could be a person worthy of contemplation, which perhaps I saw as the real difficulty in a field of liberals decrying the evils of prison and rallying, even in the popular discourse toward abolition, the project of loving someone innocent found guilty or maimed in cold blood was just too easy; I wanted to learn how to love people through real conflict, not just of ideology or mistake, or of the obviously narrowing sphere of choice we are thrust against, but of deed and consistent material harm because otherwise, what was the point? We didn't start there though, when I opened the door on Lucretia Mott Way we dapped each other up and hugged. We caught up a little bit through mutual complaint: The Gardens were supposed to be some kind of escape, but after just a couple months he didn't see it like that no more.

"Niggas is everywhere," he said in that way Chris Rock once famously described "niggers." "Niggas really is everywhere." This lament was about the frequency of stabbings and shootings in the suburb accompanying this era of white flight; just a few doors down there was still yellow tape by the entrance to the brand-new pool area, blocking off the unused grill and still drying cement speckled with ugly pavers. We talked about how exciting it was that Ray was using the G.I. Bill now to study art for real at Temple, averse as he'd been to debt and having put off college till almost in his thirties. In his living room there was an expensive computer with a hood for photo editing, and the two cats he used to hate but fought for when his ex left right after the newness of his being home wore off. We laughed about missing the army and hating college and hating the army and dreaming of college and hating work and the exhaustion of spending time with old friends or family, the necessities of staying strapped in Philly and how, just a week or so ago, he'd gotten jumped by some young bouls at the laundromat, showing me the cut above his eye. Ray regaled me with tales of his return to hoe life post the hot throbbing loss of Dasha, how he considered suing this white girl he met online who tricked him into thinking she was Latina, until it was too late, meaning after he'd already given up the booty, that precious resource of taking time off work for STI testing, the time and money cleared from a hectic schedule in the support of first impressions. He told me how he still loved Dasha but was trying to be responsible for the future, given their not equidistant desires and career paths. And though he could no longer afford her, he told me, he was never giving up those cats.

I didn't tell him about the era where I'd been spending most of my money on a hotel far enough away that no family members could catch the bus or train there and experimenting for the first time in my life with whatever kind of drugs and falling in and out of love with someone we both used to know, Tiana from Set It Off, in the exact ratio that I was on or off whatever substances. I did not tell him that pending a DNA test I might have a daughter, which I'd discovered six months after the cutting of all ties and being threatened by her older kid's dad, how this nigga shot at me from the second-floor window—no aim—and called me a bitch a couple times, before she moved from West to North and after I'd hurt my ex's feelings with this information and my refusal of marriage or kids, never telling her why since telling her why would have meant convincing her that I had feelings and could grow tired which was a task that ran contradictory to what she'd learned on Twitter and at the university and despite this she didn't want to cut ties and she'd ask, removing her clothes by the side of the bed after coming in past midnight: "So you never wondered why she ain't invite you to her place all that time huh? You're suddenly just so naive and innocent."

I didn't say to either of them that I knew damn well she was with her kid's dad and did not care in the slightest, how perhaps this released me from a certain responsibility to care for her heart, which I had not the slightest interest in.

I told Ray about my project, and why I was interested in the man. His face, which was often his face concerning explicit matters of the hurtful past—the difference between the trite tale of *I grew up poor* and the countless specificities of having no resources during one's formative years and bad credit at seventeen for all the bills listed in your name since age eight—was scrunched into place like what I said smelled bad. For context Ray was a broke black dude from North Philly, so his own dad was trash, of course; it was part of the script. Though he would never, under any circumstances, explicate the details of how much it continued to hurt emotionally and socially, intellectually, not just economically, how much catching up would always need to be done. And all this besides, Ray's dad was just regular trash. He cheated on his mom, mostly didn't have a job, maybe did some drugs, regular shit, but he wasn't beating or raping nobody. My dad though, was not—for Ray, and I suspect for most people including myself—a human being. He was a problem. And I was starting to admit to myself that it was an interesting problem. Though I kind of didn't wanna agree that he was subhuman because it made me feel scummy and weak in my resolve toward some kind of redemptive potential for the species. So while Ray would at least play *Tekken* with and talk shit about his dad, I didn't really know how to engage mine at all, which meant I didn't know how, and wouldn't bother knowing how to engage other black men at all if the theories are to be read at face value. Cowardly. This is what I thought standing next to someone who regularly said I was their only male friend, who'd gone bald and got buff, and who, like me, had never been able to take male teachers, male authority, or male trust remotely seriously. And I think this said a lot about how we were with each other. But now curiosity and aspiration were to accede cowardice. In the intellectual world I could be different in my responsibility to others and for the first time develop the patience and long-term acumen necessary to enact minuscule change before the end of my life. I was obligated. I had debt, and fewer excuses for not realizing the truth of this. And for any savvy investigator, in some obtuse way, the man I'll call dad for the sake of clarity—who was among the acres of flesh rotting by some off-white toilet on a concrete floor—was part of this. It made me feel kind of fleshy, too fleshy in addition to just tired, so there I was. Investigating.

"When's the last time you even heard about the boul?" Ray had said, sitting at his computer. He was editing naked and seminaked glamour shots of mostly black women models in his living room. The other tabs were *Monster Hunter* speed runs and new weapon tutorial videos. Ray's art gets on my nerves sometimes, in part because it feels hypocritical to his (our?) life project and other times because of how much I enjoy looking at it or, perhaps how it reminds me of a fundamental wrongness in my own ways of seeing.

—

I DIDN'T ANSWER HIM, but the last time I had heard about the boul (the father) was the old house visit incident while Ray and I were in Baghdad. The one where he surprisingly didn't ask for money. He'd come to Glenloch wanting me to meet my other kin, family members on his side who, for the past twentysomething years of life he'd neglected to mention. Allegedly, he was proud that I had joined the army, though no more interrogative of this pride than the average bear. The strangest part though, as told by my little brother, was that he followed him to school and kept askin about me. But Juju Man couldn't tell him shit because Juju Man didn't know shit about me either.

I had heard from Popop who had heard from my brother while he was talkin to my sister that my dad was lookin for me. Mind you, I had never met this nigga before, and so "lookin for you" sounds like a threat at first, and certainly, there were all these too-familiar iterations of him percolating around what I might later learn to call mythology—this vague memory of a kinda

fine, tall black man ducking through the door one
Christmas bearing gifts into our old roachy apartment
that I'm certain somebody or some world had had to
tell me at some point—or it coulda been pure fantasy
from some movie I'd watched about Idris Elba being
somebody's dad and also maybe a DJ? Perhaps some
role he played that must have infiltrated my psyche too
deep. But I thought of one of my stunt double friends
who had met Idris Elba and said he was a complete dickhead, which tamped down my expectations. I mean, the
description was rough, like Idris was trash according to
said friend, and since the laying bare of those facts I
have to actively forget in order to find joy as usual watching *Luther*. Not having been home in six years though,
the talk about my dad having dropped by swallows up,
to my surprise, all the normally (in)formal questions
about my sex life and whether I was messin with anybody (a wife) or not (kinda gay). No one asks me about
the deployment I had just been released from, just
like no one asks specifics on the returns from prison.
I had barely walked into the same-lookin ass house in
Frankford with the birch-beer-stained glass table, feet
squishing along the floor and nudging another meow-
ing calico cat off me before folks start talkin bout "ya
dad." My sister had started talkin like this about Mom
too, like "ya mom," every time she referred to her, even
while she was in the room which meant there was beef
at the level of blood spilling. Apparently, they'd had a

knife fight a few weeks ago that my brother had to break up; Mom still had a bandage on her arm. She had been begging my sister to let her watch the baby and, when my sister relented and ran to the store, she comes back to Mom absent and the baby lying like a little lump on the floor.

My grandfather was in good spirits. The Temptations were blaring on the radio, and everybody was simultaneously watching *Law & Order: SVU* on the TV and talkin loud over both sounds about how my dad was lookin for me. I sat down slowly and started eating a chicken cheesesteak and a regular cheesesteak at the same time—because I missed this, and was starving, and they only cost $3.00 each (up from $2.00 via inflation over several years)—I joked with my mother, brother and sister about everything I'm learning in polite society not to joke about, like experience.

"I can't remember ever lookin for that nigga," I say. But with all the narratives and the discourse though, and Freud and them looming over school I have to consider whether I am now lying, whether education has taught me, more than anything, to lie. It was always this thing, having become the pseudo-educated one in the family, whether I was to believe all the shit proper folks of all identifications said or wrote about us, or whether I would believe what I felt, what my people said in real life, my people who would be shot tryna cross the threshold of the university, despite any kind of representational war waged in their name. Though I'd feel like a fraud either way.

My brother and them was like, "Yeah I don't ever remember you talkin about or askin for boul any more than I asked for my pop which was absofuckinglutely never. Who got time for that kinda shit? Ya dad," he said, pointing to our sister, "lookin like Bunk from *The Wire* and shit, came around with money sometimes so that was nice."

Was I lying already? Do I keep or leave the gerunds? Is this how I actually talk? Why does this feel better than success? My family makes me hyperconscious. How serious I take blood relations and where boundaries get drawn and who is dying for the fact that I am the only one that graduated high school and didn't hug nobody before I went to Iraq. And hadn't I had long since exhausted my energies on the black boy qua father genre or the black boy qua mother genre, the black Man qua the world genre now looking over my shoulder demanding an articulate though no less circumscribed response?

I did look for this nigga a little bit though, on the internet where one finds anything else. My brother said his name was Rell and he look like a young boul actually, kinda soft and short and light-skinned with hang-time-less A.I. braids. My mom was gettin on my nerves eatin off both the cheesesteaks after she had said explicitly, though groggy and sobering up before I went to the corner store in the first place, that she ain't even want nothin to eat. The real reason I had showed up after all this time gone, post my dramatic exit as a teen and then working at Game Stop, Home Depot, three different restaurants, as a grunt for contractors, at the Dollar Tree, and then, finally, as a medic in the army, an emergency department tech, a nurse's aid and graduate student, was ostensibly for the purpose of writing a book. A memoir. I would get to the bottom of all manner of interpersonal, intersubjective, traumatic, structural, geopolitical, stereotypical, historical, and affective obliteration captured in what Saidiya Hartman calls the afterlives of slavery: "skewed life chances, limited access to health and education, premature death, incarceration and impoverishment." Despite the fact that my mom and them already had hood names and it was more fun to just talk shit with them and eat cheap, dopamine-smashing foods until a doctor (quite soon) would tell me I needed to stop. Doctors would tell us so much. I was reminding everybody that I was recording when Juju Man really went in on the story about my dad.

"So this nigga came outta nowhere, right." Juju likes to stand up with knife hands for emphasis when he talks. "Lookin all weird and shit, and he little, so I thought it was a little kid or somebody tryna rob me or somethin, so I turn around wit a stank face on like what the fuck is boul doin walkin so close. And mind you I'm walkin to school, early as shit in the mornin already mad so I'm like 'Yo, you good bro?' and he was kinda polite, but it was like I scared him or somethin. Grown ass man. I gotta say I really did not expect this nigga to be so soft. Apparently, he musta seen me come out the house and was like shy and waitin for a opportunity or some shit, so he was like, 'I'm sorry. Do you know my son, Joseph?' And at this point I hadn't seen you in like five years bro, nobody had, so I asked this nigga like 'Joseph, my big brother?' and he kinda just nodded." Juju Man squinched up his face, confused at the man or the memory. Everybody laughed, but especially my sister. Juju went on. "So I was like 'Naw man, I ain't seen him for a while you gotta ask somebody at the house bro, I'm bout to be late for school.' Then I turned around and kept walkin but get this, he kept walkin behind me. I'm like 'Nigga the house over there,' so I pointed and gave him that look and he just waved at me like a fuckin creep."

I was still laughing but also trying to properly decipher the story. "Okay," I said. "That's real strange but why would he show up outta nowhere now anyway?"

Juju Man sat back down. "This was years ago, still. But you know how deadbeat niggas get remorseful sometimes outta nowhere."

"He ain't ask yall for no money?"

"Yall trippin," my sister said.

"These niggas trippin," Mom said. "On old shit."

"You was trippin, you was the one fuckin boul," my brother said.

"True," Mom said. "That's right shit it was good at the time too."

Mom kept stuffing her face with my cheesesteaks, nodding. She scowled whenever I looked over at her.

Juju started again. "Joey tell me you not bout to go crawlin to this nigga like, 'Father! Father! Look at me I'm smart now I go to college and read books! Will you love me?'"

They all laughed. "'Please love me Daddy!'"

I just looked at him for a second until the chuckling collapsed. "I never told you this Juju," I started to say, "but you was trash on the court before you got sent away and broke that nut ass leg."

My sister chimed in, "I do still got that video of him dunkin on you though Joey lemme—"

"Old shit," I said. "I had on flip-flops."

Also, "Other niggas read books bro," my sister said.

"Yeah Juju," Mom said.

"Yall only read those freak ass books cause yall don't get no ass," Juju said. "Black booty chronicles and shit." He slid one of my sister's Zane novels out from under the TV.

Juju's daughter came running into the livin room crying. A roach skittered up on my scarf and I shook it off and kept eating, racing my mother to the end of the cheesesteaks, rolling my eyes at her. It was cold inside, so I kept my jacket on. Juju Man had gotten this little heater from upstairs in his room and put it in front of his two-year-old who was then rubbing her little hands together, losing heat.

"Aight little girl," my sister said, turning to her. "It's time to get ya hair done." She thanked me for the cheeseburger I brought back as she unwrapped it from the tinfoil, then took a bite before looking up at me.

"You ain't remember none of that Joey?" Mom said, excited by a superior recall. "I been told you."

"I remember something about you saying he came, yeah," I said. "But I called that number he left before, and his mom answered and nobody ever called back. Wasn't he like ten years older than you anyway? And you was twelve? Somebody shoulda killed that nigga by now." I supposed I only called outta some morbid curiosity. "You know how it's like everybody gettin killed by the Xenomorph, but you really wanna see the whole thing emerge from the darkness. How there's somethin really satisfying in that?" I couldn't tell if I had thought or said the last part out loud. The distinction, since returning from Baghdad, had been blurring more often than I could stand.

Everybody stared at me, silent for a few seconds.

"What?" my sister said.

"A couple years older I think," Mom said.

"Boul is fuckin gross," my brother said, feeding the baby cereal from the bottle.

"Maybe we should just kill him," I said. I looked over to my mom, chuckling. "Yall know his last name?"

My mother looked up and over at the wall, pondering the question. There was a huge R. Kelly poster across from the TV next to a portrait of a lion, and a wood-framed suede portrait of MLK. A few months ago there was a concert and my grandmother would not stop talking about how great R. Kelly was in person, and I was reading that "808s & Heartbreaks" essay for like the fifteenth time in preparation for teaching it to Ivy League undergrads. My own kids came runnin into the living room then, chasing after one of the dogs chasing after the cat chasing after something smaller. GodRaptor69 hit the edge of the table, cried a bit, then came to me for a boo-boo kiss, and started running again after giving me a crooked smile and thumbs-up all within thirty seconds. From that point on it was hard to focus, stressed out as I was regarding what his mother would say about the scar and how to explain it in court. They slid across the kitchen floor grabbing the poodle's legs, pinning her to the ground as she licked and nibbled their little baby bodies.

"We gotchu Cassie!" they yelled. Cassie threw her head back in surrender.

"You sure that dog ain't gonna bite them kids?" my mother said.

I turned back to her. "You should be more worried about them bitin the dog. Anyway," I said. "Why—"

"I'm sorry baby," Mom interrupted, looking at that last piece of regular cheesesteak. "You gone eat that?"

"I'm surprised you ain't take it when I went to the bathroom," I said.

She unhinged her jaw to eat the last bite, like some kind of dragon. "I was bein polite," she said.

Juju Man stood up again as our sister subdued the baby, same time her kid ran into the room screaming and my brother scooped the boy up instinctively, standing by the door like a light-skin black Muslim sentinel with this long, slimy onion stuck in his beard from a burger. And while my sister had converted, we'd left alone the question of faith for his part, then and into the future, forgetting most of the time to consider whether he'd staked his first serious religiophilosophical position. His daughter looked way up to him from the loveseat across the room, frowning as if everything she couldn't express was wrong, and whining "Daddy, Daddy" as she pointed to her braids and he kept holding Little Juju still, lest the boy squirm out of his arms and start tossing glasses of juice and lighters, flinging cats and sprinting out into the streets yelling with the spaghetti strainer over his head and Juju, for his part, tried to soothe them both saying "It's okay baby it'll be over soon" to his daughter and otherwise informing the room and held child he was "just checkin for snakes out here."

Then he turned to me. "Joey, you said you called him before, why don't you try callin again?"

Searching for the number, I made goofy faces at his

daughter, who sometimes confused me for her daddy. Tons of text messages had poured in which I'd promised to respond to more promptly one day, and I lingered on their one-sidedness, both from my end, toward a potential lover and on the other, from bill collectors and exes, fake friends in proximity or real friends who'd since moved away, CHOP appointment alerts, the lawyers, late-night convenience calls, corny jokes from The Old One or The Long One and their friends, one who calls me Mr. Cookies cause I wouldn't give her no cookies when she came over for dinner cause she didn't wanna eat no dinner and I figured, rather than dig into these contexts it might be easier to try calling the father again. When I hit dial and the phone started ringing, everybody got quiet for a few seconds, even Stabler from *SVU*. It rang six times before an older black woman picked up.

"Hello," she said.

"Hello," I said. "I'm looking for a man named Rell Grant. I'm his son." The "his son" part felt off, but I didn't have time to think more seriously about relation at the moment, or to explain to this stranger why I was calling her phone outta nowhere asking for some nigga I barely knew under the assumption that she really knew him or would admit to it. Should I have said I think he's my father? Was there a language I could use to do this that didn't establish relation at all?

"You got the wrong number honey," she said.

I archived the call.

Mom was gettin more animated and suggested we look online. The first Google hit was a mugshot of a tiny black man, light-skinned with braids, named Tyrell Emmanuel Grant, or T.E.G., a set of initials which I quite liked the mouthfeel of. I showed the picture to Mom on the opposite side of the couch, sliding her can of strawberry Day's soda out the way and waiting for her to shrink the lump of cheesesteak in her cheek; she leaned in and squinted, brother and sister following.

"Yo that look like a mug shot," my brother said. An expert, as the most recently incarcerated person through a long line of imprisoned folks in our family was his daughter's mom, who had been doing a bunch of credit card fraud and got caught fighting this other girl at The Gallery.

"What else would it be?" I said.

My mother snatched the phone. She slowed down in a way I'm not used to her doing sober, easing into the image. "Yup. That's him," she said. "Nigga look exactly the same."

My brother started laughing. "Damn Joey I coulda told you that. That's just how that nigga looked when he followed me to school."

We all laughed and laughed till my sister, quieter than the rest, turned back to my baby niece's hair.

I must have been thinking about consistency. The

should-be shattering consistency of information gleaned like this by some kind of capture, the way we only know what we know from prison and health records and I couldn't think anything except how soon I'd be able to find my brother and sister here too, or their kids, forever frozen in circumstance next to Ganny and Popop, our mother and all the aunts and uncles, play cousins and former teammates, out-of-work barbers and EMTs from Bridge Street, that guy who used to live in the garage next to our house and of course Greg, snatched up from under the El selling bean pies and forced to confess the sins of social impoverishment, which are ultimately whatever the officer needs them to be; the weight of my chest suggests that this has started to have physical effects on my body and I spiral about what kind of relationships my children will have to this world. How will they enter the prison system ahead of or lagging just behind the siblings? And what would I do about it? It's cut short though, the thinking, by my mother who, sensing something off in me, turns her head and forces a smile.

"Joey," she says. "I'm so proud of you."

And I recognized then that this is an image she needs to see, that I've helped her and the other people who need me for one thing or another see, and despite the utter mistrust in myself and pride more generally, I did the easy thing, which is also the dishonest thing, and I fixed my lips into a smile for her.

\* \* \*

LATER, I SENT THE image and name to an activist friend of mine who likes to stalk people on the internet.

Siblings say I look like him, I wrote.

Wow, they reply. You don't look nothin like the dude. But the records are uhhh many. There's a longer pause, the text bubble floating there in anticipation. Well, you both got tiny ears I guess.

There's a screenshot which captures a fraction of the man's life and some chunks of the lives he's impacted.

Rape of a child.

Agg. Ind. Assault W/O Consent

Unlawful Contact With Minor—Sexual Offenses

Sexual Assault

Incest

Etc.

He's currently at Holmesburg, my friend continued. But didn't they shut that place down?

The rest of my texts were from Ray and Wais and her boyfriend about how I was slackin and needed to get on *Monster Hunter* immediately. Others are my kids' moms about money or exchanges at the police station.

Apparently still open. But you know they closed that WoW skating rink next to K-Mart on The Boulevard?

—

NEVER HAD I EVER planned on returning home. I went on explaining to Ray how Juju Man had described that scene of Rell following him to school asking about me, how he had one of those strange faces stuck between little boy and grown ass man and to top it off an even more feminine walk and habit of hand gesturing than little-boy me, which still sometimes made Juju Man uncomfortable. He didn't have to tell me this, but I was reminded because I had tried to hug him before I deployed to Iraq and he pushed away from me like I was being weird and then we both just cried for a bit, not touching. But of course he was a bit of a creep (my dad) if the justice system had anything to say about it, and the justice system be sayin a lot of shit I don't or shouldn't agree with about me too. After calling back then, I was frustrated by the too-fulfilled expectation that he was using some woman's phone. It would have been a great time for my assumptions to be wrong.

I kept explaining all this to Ray. How I was sitting in the old livin room with my mom and them, just talking shit and something came up about everybody's dads: mine, my sister's and my brother's, respectively. My sister's dad was basically like Ray's dad, kinda trash, but came around sometimes, gave her money, told her he loved her at least six or seven times in her life and introduced her to other siblings. How the information we'd sought resulted in an hour-and-a-half conversation about our ears, how Rell looked exactly the same as even my mother remembered.

Complaining to Ray about the pride thing he's like "Yeah, everybody proud they can ask you for money now"; we laughed and filled our collective Cash App requests. I explained how Rell was at Holmesburg, bout to turn fifty-three, and in there for multiple counts of murder, manslaughter, child molestation, etc. and how even though the facts were as I expected them, they felt different than I had expected them to feel; the confirmation and its source were more frustrating than uncertainty. Of course, everybody was stealing, doing drugs, beating and raping kids, and we were always involved in some shit that was categorically "bad" to anyone on the outside, but everybody always denied that shit, especially to each other and ourselves. Like even to this very day, after watching my mom and them fuck johns in the living room, or my step pop beat them and do crack everyone acted like it never happened, no matter how much the kids cried or complained. But in this odd moment it was like centuries of gaslighting by the elders was finally being confirmed through the justice system and I could hardly stand it. Or myself. Maybe I wanted to know, but to know in a different way, like having someone I loved be honest with me instead of the state, this amorphous and diabolical entity that we're all supposedly opposed to.

And so, trained (or forced?) as I was to see opportunity in every manner of misfortune, I thought to myself, damn, this is a book. I would go and see Tyrell in jail, ask him about the experiments they were doing there, prolly get funding or at least reimbursement for my gas, and in the process I might actually learn something about myself and my family too. I explained all this to Ray, and he just kept shaking his head.

"So ya dad is basically R. Kelly," he said, still working in Photoshop. I sat on his couch petting the friendlier of the two cats.

"Well," I said. "No, not necessarily, but I see what you mean. The power and scope thing is a little different." The difficulty in being precise but not apologetic.

"Maybe," he went on. Then he walked over to the frigerator and got a bottle of aloe juice so tall you had to lay it down on the shelf to fit it inside. He offered me one, but looking at the pulp flitter around in there while he guzzled his was nasty. It was the regular flavor too, not even pineapple. And he knew I had a thing with pulp. He finished drinking, and almost started over. "So ya pop is basically R. Kelly, and you gonna drive all the way up in the Northeast to talk to this nut ass nigga and maybe write a book about it."

"Basically," I said. "Yeah. It's for work."

"Well you have fun with that," Ray said, turning his body away from mine.

And I wanted to respond to him, but I wasn't sure how to do it without argument. It was getting late and I had to pick up the kids anyway, so we hugged and I promised him we'd all get on some hunts later, once everybody went to sleep. That night, I never got online. Him and Wais and B went hunting in a group of three. They were hitting me up on the group chat heavy, talking shit.

Where this nigga Joe at?

You know he got fancy now and shit he dreamin in Literary

All them kids prolly killed him

Ayo Joe, wake up bitch nigga come get these hunts

Yall aint right you know he old and prolly sleep now

This was the first night Tierra came over, so I didn't respond to anything.

ANYTIME SOMETHING HAPPENS I consider, if only in the few milliseconds before the pangs of guilt, shirking my responsibility entirely: the birth of children, emails with vague or direct questions posed to me, lovers who need, and for certain, work. But somehow I just don't always have the fuck it in me. So I send the Cash App requests and apologize profusely both for myself and for other people and all the things that make me me and you you in the hopes of avoiding family court or the desiccation of my nieces' and nephews' hungry little bodies or, just as tragic, a sexless future. I grab the last pair of extra-large gloves and gown and slide into the trauma bay right through the flock of residents who mostly watch and start slicing off another brown boy's clothes. The strangest part is that even though I'd seen him come in just minutes ago I must have been gripped by the most powerful denial of my life. So I regret the double take necessitated while feeling up the arm and attaching the BP cuff. *I've felt this arm before because I have touched this person before and we have shared a closeness hard to forget and the warmth is exceptional and dense and is this the left or right arm blacked out* and the thought terrifies me beyond the reach of each grade school body I've dug into, every "bullet bag" with tourniquet or transfusions hopelessly applied to flesh parts in crisis, and I think I've made a mistake in sensation and place and time and the room is crowded with everyone shuffling around and giving orders and as the pants come off a chocolate Otis Spunkmeyer muffin half flat falls out of the Brunello Cucinelli jean pocket the way wads of money or coke or weed or wallets with photos of young children in them or cracked iPhones with nudes of people you know or maybe I'm delaying the inevitable when I get a glimpse of the face half-recognizable, but too fully known being the person who for long as we knew each other kept calling me his only male friend, the bullet having ravaged the left side of his face and he's awake, thrashing, which is good I think, *this is good*, and just like every time a loved one comes through the doors I tell no one and hold my breath. Ray does not look exactly the same. My hands moving faster now applying the BP cuff, inserting the IV, raising the stretcher, weaving in and out of people's arms and legs for supplies, I consider that last we spoke he said "Aight, love you man" and I did not say it back, rushing off the phone for some urge which once satisfied could never be satisfied.

Another man is dragged into the bay just then by police, banged up and weeping, no, a boy of about sixteen though still fucked up and crying for his mother and they bang his head against the stretcher and force his face down. The boy is mad thin and we divide our attention between him and Ray. In the rush to sedation, a cop relays the scene to a new doc: The boy and a couple others tried to rob Ray at Broad and Olney; those who got away still had Ray's gun and another, shot, was already dead, more dead than the heart attack a few patients prior who warranted, for any potential loved ones and our collective gains in proficiency, a feigned attempt at resuscitation.

We strip and assess the boy as the cops frisk him, turn his jeans inside out and uncuff him so we can remove his shirt as he lulls into a Propofol nap and we discover, much to the chagrin of some and relief of others, that aside from the lumps in his face, some combination of Ray fighting back and the police having grabbed him, the boy is fine, if *fine* describes a certain kind of summer Tuesday. Downstairs gathering the blood I think that Ray will be fine, or I imagine him coping the way one does, a beautiful man, though survived, maimed into stillness. A white boy who lost one arm and one leg like Edward Elric while we were deployed had taken it well, extraordinarily some said, given the fact that he got his wife pregnant immediately after; in pictures he smiles with the bland force of virility. Ray joked that this boy had single-handedly saved the masculine form, rekindled us with value into the twenty-first century.

In the basement there's another tech taking a small body into the morgue. We exchange the nod and go our separate ways and I hear him say "Damn this jawn full as shit" from down the hall as I wait with my little blood slip. We verbalize the information to each other, Vea, the lab tech, this older Jamaican woman who I usually joke with: time, date of birth, blood type and sign. Rushed, I must seem to her, which is also another term for rude, skipping past colloquialisms, I can't stop trembling. Tremble like the first time I'd ever gone to the blood bank on my own, afraid even to speak out loud lest I forget the quick and efficient protocols of the hospital form, those gestures that demand confidence or promise embarrassment. Vea frowns at me when I grab the bag and turn around, almost running back upstairs. But why? I don't imagine this minor intervention as the lifesaving mechanism, nor do I obsess over the seconds and, when I return, the bay is cleared out and he's being rushed up to surgery. A trauma nurse grabs the blood with a nod and a thank-you.

THE MOST IMPORTANT THING we built in Baghdad was the network. We got a few thousand feet of ethernet cable from the Pakistani dude who sold suits to soldiers that had only seen suits on *The Office*, every episode passed around on a sticky black hard drive. One day we'd all be home and every other nigga would be a broke entrepreneur with a fade and a Mustang; or they'd be K–12 teachers, civilian medics or house-husbands, emotional support dog owners or that dangerous combination of young and hoeish drunks in their first apartments; some would be home owners, gun owners, or cat owners; a few would have farms; others would be nurses or physician assistants or perpetual students or in recovery. Plenty would be dead. Or worse, poor again. Either way, this nigga at the only two-story building on base, the Pakistani guy who kept telling folks different names every day, sold suits and ethernet cable by the bundle. He also had Xboxes and PlayStations, yo-yos, rugs, *Pokémon* cards, *Yu-Gi-Oh!* cards, *Magic the Gathering* cards, graham crackers and pretty much whatever you could have asked for the day prior and in very black fashion, we'd joked about privately, reminded us of the many benevolent hustlers we knew in North Philly happy to procure and resell anything *but* drugs, the "fell off the truck" types whose opportunism was, though mandated by incredibly savage external circumstances, "nonviolent," who would frown upon risking harm on anyone else in their efforts to get what needed getting, some cross between Freeway's "If my kids hungry snatch the dishes out ya kitchen" and conscious rappers who, despite incredible goofiness, have continued to carry the torch of Dudley Do-Right into our collectively burning future with a Coke and a smile. One time the PX was out of Twizzlers and he sold me some at a small markup. Eating the Twizzlers with one hand, me and Ray carried the heavy ass roll of ethernet cable with the other and knocked on Burgos door. He came out wearing this knock-off purple Savage Fenty–like robe before it was cool. It was open, with plain white briefs underneath. He'd never been able to grow chest hair or a beard. Me and Ray looked at him, then each other, and then at him.

"Okay," I said. "You tryna help us take these *Call of Duty* ass whoopins across the whole platoon?" It wasn't necessarily true, of course. Ray and I were great at *Call of Duty* together, untouchable honestly in this band of all males unit, but we spent much more time playing co-op on *Borderlands* or *Little Big Planet*.

Burgos looked a little confused at first, then he mustered the once-dormant excitement he'd been saving for an invitation to a social group. "Hell yeah bro!" he said.

Neither Ray nor I loved the word "bro," and Ray had strong feelings about the word "nigga," which had already been the fulcrum of my vocabulary. Ray used to say he never said "nigga" like that until he was around *us* niggas—meaning me and the other niggas in our platoon, mostly from Philly—but now he had been cursed with the affliction and could not stop. And though Ray and I loved each other, he despised the others in our midst with a passion, the twenty or so in our whole battalion, with a rather unsurprising enmity. It was a trauma response I supposed, wherein Gillie and Harris, Williams and Robinson, Thomas and Greene, Brown and Allen, Adams and Davis reminded him too much of having to fistfight on the corner of Allegheny, in the parking lot of Church's Chicken, on the 56 bus, on the El, on the subway, at school, in the schoolyard, at the cookout, etc. Now we were all carrying at least one gun, temporarily, and there had only been two fistfights, both of which, predictably, were over the scarcity of food and sex. The white dudes were no-brainer villains who didn't qualify as potential friends. For as much as Ray hated the other black dudes, the whites, or those meth city chicks, the snow honkeys, depending on the day, were not worthy of life. That Ray bludgeoned one of them with a metal chair for maybe fifteen minutes because he accidentally knocked on our door was not included in the total fight count since it was not technically a contest of equals or an exchange of blows and, more importantly, nobody snitched. Blowback was the same crackheads and convicts stuff they already thought about us collectively.

Then there were the Rican dudes from home like Burgos and Romero who I went to high school with and were either on neutral racial terms (Burgos) or just black (Romero). Burgos though was a nerd, not the kind of nerd like us, who liked things back when there was social risk associated with those desires, but Burgos was a nerd who knew how to *do* things, who made things. This, combined with the fact that he was our 25B IT guy and also spent most of his downtime playing games, made him the obvious link.

"Hell yeah, bro," he said again before Ray shook his head and patted Burgos on his.

"Whoa there horsey," Ray said. "We're gonna get it done but you gotta calm down."

Burgos slapped Ray's hand away. "Fuck outta here man."

I broke up the goofy argument they tried to have afterward. We didn't have a drill, so we went back to the shop and got one before starting the job with Harris and Gillie's shipping container, both of whom came to the door in loose old-man boxers with the single button where one's dick sometimes hangs out. Burgos glanced at their TVs and systems to gauge where the hole should go and went around back while Ray kept asking why they would wear those boxers and whether or not it hurt your balls when you ran in shit like that. Gillie flagged Ray off and Harris turned around with a tsk and both said versions of *Come on with that gay shit all the time nigga what the fuck.*

"Thomas, get ya little boyfriend," Gillie said.

"I already got him," I said. "Things are secure here. Why don't yall focus? Is you niggas high?"

Harris laughed. "Every nigga you encounter in the wild ain't high nigga what is you talkin about?" He put his clothes on. "Always trippin."

They was high as shit. We figured that since Gillie and Harris were next best at the game after Ray and I it might be nice to expand the fighting with them fast on our side; it would be the first time we'd be able to do sixteen-player matches, and if we disagreed on pretty much everything else, we certainly agreed that the white boys were not to be permitted victory, especially not the leadership. The pleasure of creating the network was half discovered in the drilling of holes; those shipping containers, whatever they were really made of, trapping heat and trapping cold, their insulation just a little better than the apartment buildings where we'd all grown up, were flimsy. There was a strict pleasure in popping through their flesh with the drill, the bit of resistance, then crack and sliding into the other end of a world. This world was one where we forced recreation under conditions otherwise averse to pleasure. There was of course, of course, a no-sex rule undergirded by the assumption that pregnancy or STDs would be a troop-readiness problem; no sex between men or between women, at least not when Louie and eventually Robinson got kicked out for suckin a little dick. The dude Robinson was goin down on acted surprised when our platoon sergeant came in and flicked the light on, like a cat stumbling across a glistening cucumber and mistaking it for a snake.

"Oh shit! Oh my god!" he'd said, like he wasn't just about to cum.

And that was another problem with that increased lack of privacy, the tents we were holed up in waiting out the waiting in Kuwait or Al Asad mostly covered in grime and sweat that somehow, when horny enough, smelled delicious in the most precise way. Anyway, the dude getting head, Tyson, was the third person to kill himself after we got home. When he came into the trauma bay that day I had to pretend I didn't know him as everybody talked shit. Louie wasn't working at the time and I never told him about it, just like he never got a severance package from the U.S. Army. Myriad other rulings about the potential conditions for fun were also espoused and written down in doctrine, but this didn't foreclose completely the possibility of playing digital games. I think in part this was because of their relative newness, the inability of folks to figure out the exact ways to regulate or analyze even, such a rapid cultural change in pleasures, unless of course, simply stating that it was "good" or "bad" in direct relation to a preceding aesthetic form. The man I reported to directly was this husky E-6 named Torres who spent all day playing *Animal Farm* in his single room and sabotaging shit to keep the junior medics on our toes. He never went out on route clearance missions like us, and the one time he did someone died. He liked to talk shit about how he could still outrun anybody in a two-mile despite the beer belly and he could. During our only physical fitness test we took in Baghdad he smoked everybody, including this one white boy who had a heart attack and was told to get the fuck up and keep pushing. Also died. Importantly, we were not going to connect SGT Torres to the network though because while not white, he was even more adherent to authority in its proper form than anyone we'd ever met. He was also a dickhead and, just as bad, wasn't playing *real* games anyway. My only fistfight in adult life had been against this nigga, with the other medics anxious to jump in and grab some blows.

All this aside, Gillie and Harris came with us to help set up the rest of the platoon. Burgos left us with the cable and went to talk with his soon-to-be wife high school sweetheart on the phone. Gillie and Harris passed a blunt back and forth as we shuffled through the sand and rocks in the daytime, simultaneously watched but invisible the way negroes in space work and wondering how war could possibly have become so tame and regular for the aggressors who are also the aggressed upon, all passing a blueberry-flavored Otis among us and snatching moist clumps into our mouths. I wanted to hit the blunt, but I was afraid, not just of the asthma that I had to lie about to join the army in the first place, which almost killed me every time we had to do a two-mile run, but the puritanical judgments I held about drugs that I was only then, if ever, really getting over. Since everybody we knew growing up was fucked up beyond all recognition—FUBAR, they now called it—most days of the week, day, month, and year, I held as my most esteemed position and model for success a complete abstinence concerning drugs and alcohol and somehow, in this, still had the nerve to pretend I was better than DARE. My relationship with younger siblings had already been tarnished by the way I chastised them for smoking and drinking in their teens, yelling that they would end up just like our mom, just like our dads, just like our grandmothers and grandfathers, all our aunts and uncles lying dead or dying or burdens needing then to be raised and catered to by their own children to whom they've given no succor through the formative years of our lives.

Succor would be taken.

We traced paths to each of our dwellings and buried the wire under sand and rocks, stacking our relations to each other deep underground and out of sight, saving the best for us, by us. Other soldiers, especially from different units, stared on in amused contempt, but we did not care. Some random lieutenant approached us and asked why he smelled weed and Gillie stood at attention.

"Sir, I think that is your racism talking, sir," he said.

The lieutenant seemed shocked at the recognition for a few seconds, then he smiled. "Fuck you, you dumb little nigger," he said, and walked away.

And we were all better for this version of honesty, cracking up. Harris was like, "Did this nigga just call you a little nigger?"

"Not a regular nigga," I said, "a particularly little nigger. He young boul'd you."

"Dunked on you," Ray said, with the universal over-the-doorframe gesture known to negro males the world over.

"Fuck outta here," Gillie said, "I'll whoop boul ass outta uniform."

"That's why he wearin the uniform," Harris said.

Ray passed the muffin. "Whoop him like a little nigger?" he said in a mousy white-nerd voice.

We all laughed, mocking the lieutenant, choking on muffin.

"All jokes aside though," Gillie said. "Ain't this blue-berry flavor kinda trash?"

GILLIE TOOK TO HUSTLING when we got home. I'd hit him up for mushrooms and acid, sometimes coke, but mostly molly. Drunk off Cuervo and high off pills, he was the first to kill himself, having crashed his black Charger into a tree; we all stared at his body until the family arrived, his wife and all six kids sprinting into the department past security screaming how they did, the kids, and a few of them who remembered me, kept calling this a bitch ass hospital and saying, "Sergeant Thomas why you ain't do nothin man! Help my dad! How you even work for these people?!" And his wife, Keisha, who had also joined the army later, became sud-denly calm, accustomed.

"I knew it," she whispered. "I fuckin knew it," she cried real slow. We hugged and she went on, "He loved you, you know that? He really missed yall."

I stood there embarrassed about how lazily I'd maintained our connection, how dumb I was thinking of myself as better than him. How this was always going to happen.

THEY ADMIT THE BOY who robbed Ray to Med Surg on Tower 6 with police escorts paid overtime to sit with him. When things quiet down and the bodies are moved and the nurse managers have gone home and the bay is empty I walk in on everybody and they mom twerkin to "Flipside" at the part where Freeway is like "bad bitches get scooped like Häagen-Dazs" and I'm struck by how smoothly Lise gets her long ass leg right up on the code cart—is this what Arthur Jafa meant by black virtuosity?—and D is filming the whole scene and Uma is climbing into the camera rhythmless, and it's all activating a deeply shameful desire in me, like when I sat butt naked and clear-eyed masturbating to that "Freek-a-Leek" music video back in 2003 after resisting the urge to do so through eleven straight viewings. "Freek-a-Leek" was also playing at Louie's last barbecue where,

after having invited me over specifically for his friend
Lucinda who was, although fine, more traditional and
less funny than Peg Bundy, I ended up making out with
this one firefighter Earl who, after us hanging out a few
times, took to politely calling me an ex-bisexual whenever we crossed paths. I could not figure out if the limits
of my desire for Earl were too tepid for him being a little too masculine and with bad breath, or whether my
own curiosity had peaked as I drove to Lucinda's house
at 1:00 a.m., one friend texting me like well, how many
women have you had sex with where you didn't actually
want to? And instead of saying "way too many" I just
thought, *Yes, a very fair question.* And so of course Earl is
here too, in one of those too-tight dark blue fire rescue
shirts, bis and tris bulging and beard grown in after having dropped off a less urgent patient who sprained their
ankle and called 911.

He comes to give me a hug. "What's up wit my
favorite ex-bisexual?" he says just loud enough for me
and Lise to hear, both of us laughing.

Pac comes on: "First off fuck yo bitch and the click
you claim!" Everybody rap-yelling along.

Lise walks up and is like "Ask that hoe ass nigga
bout Tierra!"

Their faces make clear that there's nothing to say
about it and besides,

"You claim to be a playa but I fucked ya wife!"

Earl mostly wants to know if we all still playin ball on Sundays at that gym up Northeast, and when I say yeah, of course, he asks if Ray gonna be there and I stand frozen for a little bit before walking out of the bay, way too quiet.

LOOKING AT THE PATIENT screen overwhelms me with more fury than usual. I think this fury is composed, in part, by the material conditions of people's lives and in part by starvation. It doesn't help that I know so many of these people, either by blood relation or the repeated offenses of being ill, which are really just the repeat offenses of being poor, which is correlated too strongly with being not white, though in this world, in this country, in this neighborhood especially, with being black. How could something so obvious and boring still be this infuriating? The lives awaiting them after the hospital would be spent scavenging for coin under the El, dodging Capital One and Citizens Bank, Chase Family and Chase Disney Debit and Wells Fargo, getting berated on the daily by proper citizens, waiting in line for hours for "benefits" and guilt trips, stashing 1800 Tequila bottles under pissy coats and sprinting outta

Wine & Spirits, rummaging through the restaurant fodder out back, being raped or otherwise beaten round the clock and outside the buy here pay here die here places for used vehicles that will break down just in sync with their bodies. Either way I'm at work and White Top is in the waiting room for innumerable complaints.

"Yo White Top!" I yell out in the waiting room. He gets up faster than he seems able and struts over to me in that wide white hat with the feather he always wears.

"Damn Joey I'm comin, chill," he says.

"Now you know damn well I was just saying it loud enough cause it's a room full of old folks and half yall niggas can't hear at all."

He slows down a little as we walk back to a room. "You better stop sayin that shit around me Joey you know I don't play all that N-word shit," he says. "Stop fuckin playin wit me Joey."

"My bad," I say. "I know niggas is sensitive. What was ya blood pressure at home?"

When we get to the room he sits down in the chair instead of the bed, and groans when I hand him the gown and hospital slippers. "You know the deal," I say.

He laughs. "Little ass kids think they get a little fuckin job and not respectin shit don't know why the fuck these kids think they can just say what they want and do what they want woulda whooped ya little ass..." he mumbles while taking off his gator shoes and placing them on top of the supply cart. "Damn Joey you gone step out so I can put this gown on?"

Embarrassed by all the burns beneath his clothes he shoos me away, though I've seen them so often it's forgettable. He's the most directly bitter about his time at Holmesburg, compared to the others, though he's also the only one currently free. He spends most of his time trying and failing to sue the state, as he still believes, despite whatever else, in the necessity of formal redress despite its unlikelihood. Being constantly mocked by lawyers and doctors hasn't entirely ruined his pride yet.

In the next room there's these three young girls with La Salle Explorers jerseys on, one of whom is lying in the stretcher mad as hell, probably a torn ligament, and the other two by her bed eating fried chicken wings and shrimp fried rice with saltpepperketchuphotsauce. The smell is everywhere, like Michelle Branch in 2001, and it seeps into my throat before I see them, through the wall, the curtain, over the lingering bleach wipes from a quick cleanup in the next room. Judging by the circumference of the wings, the slightly darker tone of the rice and the meager but delicious portion size of the Styrofoam platter, it's definitely from Penn's. Stingy ass Penn, we used to call the guy who owns that store in Logan across the street from the courts where some of the best in North Philly would come to ball and smoke, next to the Sunoco where someone got shot a handful of times every summer. The problem with Penn being stingy with portions was that the food slapped; it was one of those places where the health code violations operated at inverse proportions to the bangin ass flavor. I would not personally have gotten the wings fried hard, but these La Salle kids were into that. Last time at Penn's I was with Cee really late one night, back when we all shared a house on Smedley Street. We'd often go to Penn's for comfort, knowing it would always be open, knowing it would always be good and close to home. On this night it was empty, and Cee strolled right up to the counter like "Yo Penn lemme get a chicken and broccoli platter but don't be all stingy on the rice please! Thank you man!" And I was licking my lips in the back fluctuating between the shrimp and broccoli with baby shrimp and extra gravy or the four chicken wings with shrimp fried rice or the house special egg foo young or something else when it was interrupted by some short nigga bumping me to get my attention. I looked down at him.

"You know what?" he said. "A bitch ass faggot nigga like you wouldn't even make it in jail."

I squinted, confused. Cee was cracking up. "What the fuck?" I said. "Who—"

"I said!" the boy got louder. "A little spoiled bitch nigga like you wouldn't. Make it. In. Prison. You little bitch." He stepped to me.

"I am so fucking confused," I said, tired. "Also, why would I wanna make it in jail?"

This had been the thing I most aimed to avoid in life honestly, the thing I had constant nightmares about, visions even. Every time I'd go to visit family or friends, came home dead eyed not wanting to talk about it. I was like absolutely not. Not me. This is the thing, if I can't avoid anything else, it'll be this. And so there was clearly something right about what this boy was saying, despite the fact that I didn't know this nigga at all.

"Who the fuck you cussin at pussy?" he said, jumping at me. And here, Cee stopped laughing and stepped up a little closer to him.

"Chill," Cee said. "Chill."

The boy pulled his gun. "You chill pussy!" he said. "*You* chill!"

I sighed at the redundancy, and wondered if I woulda had my gun on me if I'd have killed this boy. Penn poked his head from behind the bulletproof glass. "Can you guys all get the fuck outta here with that. Go. Cut it out."

We all turned to walk out but the boy stepped out in front of us and then jogged off sporadically, like a squirrel who had just fiddled around with a nut and found it lacking. Me and Cee looked at each other and started laughing again. "What the fuck man," we both said. "We gotta move."

—

MAYBE I'M LOOKING TOO hard at the food, but one of the La Salle girls notices.

"Aye boy!" the guard says. "What you want some?"

I hadn't been called "Aye boy" since I was like seventeen and I'm caught somewhere between flattery and insult, trapped in the middle of Franklin Mills Mall's social stratification tryna see and be seen. I don't even have the chance to respond.

"My friend tryna talk to you," the point guard continues.

I start laughing as I get closer. "Okay," I say. "First of all, yall are children. You gotta chill."

"No he ain't say that," the forward says to her friends. "I know this nigga ain't say that."

"Nigga you chill," another chimes in. "How old is you?"

"Me chill? Girl I'm fuckin grown I'm at work if yall don't stop playin wit me—"

"If yall don't stop playin with me," the other one on the stretcher mocks me.

"Now *you* talkin," I say. "Over there with that broke ass foot." Her friends laugh. "What happened?"

"What you think," she says. "Don't try to change the subject."

"She tripped on her son toys," the guard says.

"Explosion," the forward says.

I stare at them blankly. "I already can't stand yall."

"Sit down then," the guard says.

"That's gross. Look, I got a brother why don't yall holler at him."

"Lemme see a pic," the forward says.

I show them my brother, my six-foot-ten-maybe black Israelite little brother with the massive beard.

"Okay," the guard says. "How tall is he?"

"A lot taller than me," I say.

They nod in unison.

I give the guard my brother's number without a second thought, and then I text him. Yo I gave this girl from around the corner ya number so she prolly gonna text you.

What's her name?

I don't know nigga.

Okay so how imma know?

I don't know ask her, I write. I'm at work.

In the next room White Top is asshole naked. He always takes off his underwear even though no one ever asks him to, like he's gettin a prostate exam.

"You know you not gettin no prostate exam," I say. "You coulda kept ya draws on." He ignores this as I put the blood pressure cuff on him, attaching him to the machine and pulse oximeter and taking his temperature all out of habit. "Be right back," I say. And he grunts like a baby over the thermometer in his mouth.

"Yall ain't got no food?" he says. "I'm hungry as hell in here Joey I was out in that waitin room like thirty hours."

The blood pressure cuff hasn't gotten a reading yet, it just keeps inflating and deflating. Inflating and deflating. I tell him to try and be still while I go get him some crackers and apple juice. In the pantry though, I realize how trash the snacks all look and remember that I'd picked up that semismashed Otis from Ray's pocket. I dampen a towel a little bit to wipe the blood off and fluff the muffin before walking back into his room where there's still no BP reading.

Handing him the muffin and an orange juice I'm like "This is the best we got right now man, I'm sorry. I can try to get you somethin a little better when they bring dinner around."

"Shit Joey imma eat whatever at this point," he says, tearing open the Otis.

I watch the Otis touch his lips and see his face change; he has to bite down slowly, how one does with all things at the great apex of savory but in limited supply, like love. He wants, I can tell, to make love to the Otis. He looks at me, surprised, then back at the muffin, then around the room. "Damn Joey," he says. "God damn."

"I know right? We used to eat them jawns on deployment all the time, fucking delicious."

He mumbles something through the food about the rations they had them eat back in his day, wasn't nothin like this. But I can hear another stretcher rolling in and Crocs piling up on it, so I reiterate that he needs to sit still and then restart the blood pressure cuff again before walkin out.

It's a respiratory distress, this older white lady named Miss Gracy who I used to drive back and forth to dialysis all the time from the Northeast. She's conscious still, with a nonrebreather and $O_2$ on, grasping at people like a baby looking to get picked up, the way one always does when they really need air and air is in short supply. Having moved to the nursing home a few months back after her daughter died, Miss Gracy is already in the appropriate attire for the frequent visits, and so small the length of her body is less than my wingspan. Seeing who she is and seeing me there, most everyone goes to tend to other folks except me and Uma, who've worked with her dozens of times. Miss Gracy reaches for us with what little strength she has, and Uma holds her hands for a second.

"It's okay honey," she says. "We're gonna get you feeling better real soon."

I've already attached her to the machines and started an EKG, but fear is disposed as her oxygen saturation is already on the rise, and her breathing is becoming less labored by the second.

"Thank you honey," she says, muffled behind the mask. "Thank you honey."

In the room next door I hear Louie say "What the fuck?" So I hit the EKG print button and remove the wires real quick, handing the printout, which looks fine, to Uma who reads it quickly and glances at it with boredom, says "Thanks bruh" and also turns to Louie.

Red Top's blood pressure is 256/204 and everybody's baffled. People are wondering how he even walked in here to begin with; this whole time he's been sittin there chill on his thirteenth pack of crackers and fourth Otis muffin watching Maury on TV.

"Sir, how do you feel?" Dr. G walks in quick and asks.

Red Top, still eatin the muffin, is like, "I'm good, just a little weak. Little headache it ain't about shit."

"What is he even eating?" another nurse says. "Take that away from him."

The nurse behind her whispers, "That's how these people end up like that in the first place."

I run an EKG on him which to my eyes is hardly decipherable. Dr. G sits with it a minute and a couple of the nurses get serious on him. With little else for me to do, and our privacy diminished, I step out. The La Salle girls are being nosey asking what's going on over there and telling me to tell my brother to text them back. The chicken wings are all but gone, just one remaining, and I feel the true bite of desperation thinking about its history, how Penn dug it out of that grand flowery bag at the bottom of the frigerator earlier today and plopped it in the old grease bin to the tune of sizzle, smelling like the wings do, and fried up the rice as company and before that, all the Golden Comets packed tight in their cages off Tabor Road pinned into docility before their ascendance to wings and yet, where guilt and hunger meet I've consistently camped out in the land of both and I grab an orange juice from the cooler and D walks by joking that he's about to snitch that I'm drinking it. Rasheeda, eating a whole patient meal she must have taken from someone who hadn't wanted it, the turkey with gravy and mashed potatoes, shrugs. People had been getting written up recently for that. There's another patient rolling in fast now with three medics, so me and D both run over to help, straight into the trauma bay. A child this time, a little boy, about elementary school age. He's bleeding a lot, seemingly from everywhere, it's hard to tell.

Earl, often the most composed of the medics, speaks and moves fluid. "Multiple GSWs. Nine-year-old was at the gas station with dad."

Looking at his body I think, *Damn. Through the car.* The clothes are shredded so there's little to remove. They're sticky. And the boy is limp, so as we reach around each other and pull and press and prod check and attach nodes and remove clothes it's like his limbs might come off. Once settled, where his body no longer moves from the force of our attention, you can see the bleeding, which I rush to stop, is concentrated at his groin. The penis and testicles ravaged. There's a silence when these things happen to children, unusual in its juxtaposition to the normal GSW banter of adult men riddled with bullets. No one knows what to say of the inevitability.

No one laughs, and a few cry. Trauma moves faster than ever taking him upstairs, and the monitor I've attached with him keeps falling off the stretcher. His father is on the floor by the police in one corner, screaming in pain, their cuffs at the ready, unclear whether the man is a victim or perpetrator. They're stone-faced, the police, and also bored, and I know they would have wished the father on that stretcher instead, the way most of us have grown comfortable with. Trauma whisks the boy up to surgery where later, we'll learn, he survives, if wheelchair and colostomy bound for a shorter-than-deserved life.

The trauma bay doors swing open again quick with a push from Cee, sweating to death. "Yo we got the shooter," he says. "They bringin him in."

And two other cops run in carrying a man lumpen and shot. Flaccid, so that his head hangs over one of the cop's elbows. The boy's father jumps up screaming, "Imma fuckin kill you nigga you don't know who you fuckin wit imma kill you nigga!" he screams as the officers wrestle him down and cuff him. "Imma fuckin kill you nigga!" They slam his head into the floor, telling him to shut the fuck up.

There's less urgency with the shooter usually. No one knows him; no one ever knows the shooter, and I can't help but think as to whether this imposes a certain kind of loneliness or if the loneliness precedes the event itself. Does the shooting make one lonely, or does the loneliness transform the subject into a shooter?

Chickens and roads, natures and nurtures. Many dead children. Cee daps me up from the side as I reach for the shooter with my right hand, undressing him with curiosity and composure. We are in a laboratory, not a barrel.

Cee whispers to me, "Tell me why I just locked this nigga up a couple months ago but he got off. Who pulls a fuckin Uzi at a gas station with a kid around? Niggas is really outta control now man. And you know they bout to look at me crazy for shootin his dumb ass."

M E AND CEE USED to play ball together in high
school. Well, he used to play and I kind of got
dragged along as average, athletic, and tall. My lack of
confidence or work ethic holding me back from anything like great. In those days I was angrier, I think.
Have Cee tell it, the first time he saved me was in a
pickup game at the school gym. Class wasn't much
worth attending, so we'd always be in the gym hoopin
most every period except for lunch, always wearin ball
shorts under our Dickies no matter the weather, because
you never knew. This meant that boys from all grades
and realms of athleticism would be lined up, mingling
and talking outrageous degrees of shit while waitin for
the next run. There was this big ugly dude named Fuck
who was always there, playing ball even though football was his main thing. I never knew his real name, but
people called him Fuck because when approaching him

without awareness one might be startled upon encountering the shape and textures of his face, or pretend to be so, loudly. *Corpuscular* was a word that came to mind. The chin and jawline were excessive, far beyond a marketable attractiveness, and the skin had lumps and hills that did not constitute disability proper, but stress and poor hygiene. It pulsated. It throbbed to be popped and smacked or catered to, tended by a person with compassion, which none of us had, least of all the other athletes. It was said, and easy to believe, that Fuck lifted weights day in, day out, which explained in part why he got so much pussy cause he damn sure wasn't Guccied down to the socks neither.

Maybe I got ahead of myself. Fuck tried to post me up, mostly elbow though, no real contact, all sharp swings and angles and bust my lip. Then he was like, "Get the fuck up boy!" And I was like okay, okay, nodding my head. Cee, who was not a guard at all, brought the ball down with eyes on me and soon as he made the pass niggas on the other team were yelling to Fuck.

"Shut that nigga down Fuck, he weak as shit!"

And it's true I had just been dropped a second ago, and that before then, I'd missed two layups in a row, easy shit, one with nobody even stickin me, stumbling as I often did toward the basket, goofy, thinking about a hundred things other than the competition at hand. This time though, Fuck didn't have time to get his feet together and I was moving past him too quick. Their big man was boxed out too far from the rim and it was curtains. Just three steps away from the basket, and in the springtime of my youth, I was in the air with the rock cocked back in my right hand before Fuck's feet even left the ground. I pushed harder than normal, thrusting the ball down through the net in that way you can't miss, like dunking on a young boul court and Fuck jumped and slapped and tried to grab my wrist but it was way too late. It had to look bad judging by the sound: Niggas was losin it, all the daaaamn and yooooo, and me, of course, after hanging on the rim a bit and cutting my hands, reconsidered how I shoulda dropped my arm in elbow deep for real.

"Get the fuck up, pussy!" I said to Fuck and explicitly to Fuck with all the confidence I'd ever longed for, hanging consonants at the end like an asshole snake. Sssss.

Another dude on Fuck's team who also played football hopped in. "Damn, Fuck, you lettin bitch niggas talk to you like that?"

Fuck got up off the ground mumbling, and when he stood he was like, "This little faggot ain't shit! He can't check me!"

And I started it. It was me, technically. I had escalated the event, even though I made myself feel like it was him. "I will fucking kill you," I said. "I will fucking murder you you little bitch I swear to god," I said. I was sure not to yell, and to keep the gerunds then so niggas would know I was absolutely serious. And just as Fuck stepped to me, his face all-up-in, but not technically touching mine, the spit and sweat leaking into me, Cee, the diplomat, jumped in.

"Chill Fuck, chill. That's my boy, man, he wit me. Chill."

"You better getcha fuckin boy then Cee fore I murk this nigga. Teach em who he talkin to." Fuck was pointing, shaking his hand at me hard. "Sissy ass niggas man, go home. Who let this pussy on the court man?"

I tried to step around Cee. "Go head then," I said. "Go the fuck on then do somethin I swear to fucking god I will fuckin kill you." It felt like someone else's voice.

Someone murmured from the background, "This nigga a psycho," and "Is he bout to cry?"

The only thought in my head was ripping apart Fuck's face. But it never happened.

"Chill," Cee kept saying, "chill."

THAT WAS BEFORE WE all began teasing Cee for being a centrist, before plenty of family and friends kicked him out of their lives for becoming a cop (though this didn't stop them from asking for money). The second time, by Cee's account, that he saved me was more chill. We was at Coachella, Cee and I, the first time we'd ever left Philly together, and excited to lounge by the hotel pool and flirt, to step up stage to Childish Gambino and the

Red Hot Chili Peppers and Future and Kid Cudi. We stayed at a hotel in Palm Springs that looked the part. Pastels and palm trees, a huge open area downstairs looking out into the desert with a pool in the center and DJ spinning twenty-four hours. We got in, looked at the pool, heard the music, and went straight upstairs to change. We'd dedicate our earliest hours to the marvel of piña coladas and sundress season, the cover-ups that hardly covered up, downstairs seeing and being seen. Those years were slim, where we'd maintained our army bodies but now had grown-man confidence.

We'd only been at the pool drinking for a little bit, and chatting with a few women when I realized suddenly, as one does when drunk, that I had to go to the bathroom. Making jokes about my baby bladder Cee decided still to come with me, grabbing our drinks instead of waiting behind. The line wasn't long, and two men came out at the same time, so we were both going in, and Cee asked one of the women we were talking to to hold our drinks; she'd already used the bathroom and was just on her phone, waiting for friends. Back outside, the DJ was playing Sean Paul mixes and normally I would have been excited but started to get real dizzy, like my blood pressure was too low, overcome by nausea. I was standing up but my eyes kept closing and it felt like the temperature had gone up at least twenty degrees and Cee kept asking if I was okay and I can't remember what I said but it must have been something about lying down and then—

"I need a bath man," I said. "I gotta go lay down." And he put my arm over his shoulder.

One of the women sitting next to us was laughing, and she joked, "Yeah I can help you take a bath." She looked familiar, but I couldn't tell for sure.

I woke up the next day in the bathtub naked and dry, my head throbbing. Cee kept asking if I was okay; I'd never seen him so concerned. We'd missed all the shows for that night and I couldn't remember anything.

"You need to go to the hospital man?" he kept saying. "You think we should go to the hospital?"

"No. No. I'm good," I said. "I'm sorry." And went on apologizing the whole rest of the day.

—

ME AND CEE STILL play ball, mostly in AAU leagues, or on Sundays in the suburbs where sometimes Earl goes too, though Earl and Cee do not talk. Just like Ray and Cee do not talk, though more clearly in this instance because Cee was cheating on his girl and second, cause he became a cop, which is why most people don't talk to him no more. None of them enjoy the group chats I keep creating titled: "Why Can't We All Just Get Along," or "Why Can't We Be Friends," despite the reminders that before the army took us in we all took the police and firefighter exams every year together, desperate, and Cee just happened to be the one who went with it. I've never figured out the Earl and Cee thing other than Cee saying Earl was just a "corny ass nigga." But that was it. He looks so serious in uniform it always makes me laugh, and for whatever reason it draws more black women to him than I've ever seen in our lives. By now, it's also his longest-held job ever, and with overtime he can pay for his daughter's private school.

"Anyway," he says, turning away from the shooter. "What up man. Yall comin to the birthday party?" I don't admit that I'd forgotten about it even though his daughter and mine are best friends. He's having her birthday at The Slime Factory, and we'd all been in the group chat just a couple weeks prior complaining that this nigga would dare have his kid's party forty-five minutes away from the city.

"Yeah, we in there," I say. "We in there. You still shoulda had that shit at Sky Zone though man…"

"Ugh," he says. "Yes, you are correct, but you know who else got a say in this? Go head nigga just guess. Yes. Her mother, and it was her mother who made the executive decision that we was gonna have the party at the fuckin Slime Factory even though I'm payin for all the shit and all the kids comin in from my friends cause she ain't got none."

"Okay cool tell me how you really feel," I say, taking off my gloves and sanitizing my hands. We walk out of the trauma bay. "You should still come to Belize though," I say.

"Nigga I wish. I don't even got the money right now so I'm workin all this overtime to deal with this debt man. Support went up too and I only owe like sixty-seven thousand more right now, I can see the light."

"Imma see the light on this beach. Gonna be like $700.00 worth of light."

"Yeah yeah you have fun. What's up wit that girl, what's her name she work here right?"

"Yeah upstairs."

I can hear yelling from another room behind me.

"Fuck you! Get off me! Fuck you get off me!" someone says through the curtain.

"A little help!" D yells. "A little help yall."

In room 13, back in the corner, the woman is biting D, fangs out. He takes it well, all things considered. "Yo I'm tryna help you, you gotta chill!" he says, struggling with the last wrist restraint in his hand. A doctor and a nurse enter, the latter with a sigh.

"Goddammit her again. Get her some Propofol please," she says.

Uma quick turns out before remembering she already has Propofol drawn in her pocket all the time, which is why some people call her Sleepy Time Uma. The doc looks at her, shaking her head, but says nothing.

"Joey, tell em get the fuck off me," my mother says. "Get em the fuck off me!"

WHEN I WAS A young boul my mother was never diagnosed with anything because diagnoses were not something anyone was offered. Confusing, the whole project of imagining a stable enough relationship with health care to be made transparent, classified, calcified, and even treated; and what measures were there anyway to ensure her interior life had not been subject first to the catastrophes of the world and could otherwise be justified by chemical imbalance? What I did know was that she scared me, and that she was prone to fits of rage and hitting. That she was addicted to crack, like most of her friends, and now some of my friends. That she was treated poorly, and that she treated us poorly. As an adult I had dedicated most of the time, money and resources I could muster to her. The last time she returned from prison for stabbing this one john who didn't pay, she seemed exuberant, fat, healthy. I didn't want her to go back to Frankford again, and even she at that time could admit how such geographic slippage would turn out, so she came to stay with me. She had a new girlfriend too; this new woman made her happy. My mother who used to fuck men in the corner of my bedroom for money and who laughed when my aunt told us she was a sex worker for selling nudes on the internet; my mother who had even less respect for authority than I did, who stole whatever whenever she wanted; my mother, who scowled with hatred any time we talked about the people who look like us at my university "producing knowledge" about what it meant to look like us. My mother who was never happy, who was never safe, I remembered being happy then.

We were driving to her PO's office when she asked me, "Joey, can you teach me how to eat pussy?"

"What?" I said, turning to her, a little confused but also confused about why I was confused.

"How to eat pussy dammit," she laughed. "I done met them girls, I know you know."

And I supposed then that she was talking about the interrogations. My mother loved to show up to my house outta the blue and interrogate whoever I was dating or sleeping with as a matter of course and because we were so close in age, growing up together, I never found it strange. The gift my mother has given me was for certain not care, but the odd quality of disavowing so much of the proprietary norming we undergo in the American project and in this, a break with all conception that any woman or girl, let alone any man, would ever take care or responsibility for my well-being, that it should ever be any woman's task to tend to me, let alone purchase my flight home from college or clean my house, cook my meals, or help me survive at all; she made it clear, not by what she said or knew, but the haphazard sharing of her experience and subsequent treatment of me, how ridiculous those forms of comportment not always captured by the market or the astute liberal intellectual are, because they are not big enough political programs, and from this vantage point, neither are we, lacking in labor power or revolutionary potential at all. Whenever I dated fat women my mother asked why I *only* loved fat women, or with skinny, the inverse. Whenever I dated a man my mother would ask me about anal sex and if this was the reason my bedroom smelled weird. Whenever I dated people who were neither man nor woman my mother thought I was confused and said so, called anyone out of their gender whenever she wanted without malice, though sometimes with great confusion: first, for the freedom she saw denied to her at every angle, and later for the grand ascension, she felt, of pronouns over proteins; she'd ask after so many drag shows with her butch girlfriend what the big deal was when she made a mistake and some amalgam of middle-class persons on the street went so far and so hard toward shaming and embarrassing her for said mistake. If a woman

I dated was too old she'd ask why I was fuckin some old lady, *She got money?* She asked my ex if I was any good in bed and she was like "8/10 during the day, 6/10 at night, you gotta catch him around lunch time" and the two of them sat in the kitchen cackling and eating all my damn fried whiting. My mother was never one to lionize her own power or peculiarities nor feign her own innocence, but she underestimated how much I respected that, how rare it was in my own world and instead, she tried and failed to mother me repeatedly; it was never her skill or interest but pure sentimental imposition that we both hated, even if only I admitted it.

We was crackin up in the car though. "You really don't got no friends huh?" I said.

"Just teach me Joey, damn. Stop talkin so much shit all the time."

"You out here askin me about eatin pussy and you thought I was just bout to keep drivin the car, straight-faced? Girl, are you fucked up right now?"

"No!" she said, laughing. "But that's like all you do ain't it?"

"*Who* is givin you this information?" I said. "I really need to know ya sources." I turned off Torresdale Ave toward the prisons.

"That's confidential shit right there," she said. "Classified shit."

"You get on my damn nerves."

"Remember when you tried to kill Terrence cause

he pushed me down the steps? It was so cute you was so little tryna stab him wit that little knife."

I laughed. "No I don't remember exactly, people was always sayin it so I remember from that. Like because people kept bringin it up I was like 'Oh maybe it's true' or somethin like that. I don't remember a lot from when I was little. Like before Aunt Mina died, I remember that was your friend and she was pretty. I wanted you to have pretty friends who did things and they had things they enjoyed and were kinda weird and all that."

"Whatchu mean weird?"

"Like you know she did all the regular stuff but she had her own life." I paused for a second to think. "You know she would have a job sometimes or not have a job but she would always have somethin she wanted to do that didn't have nothin to do wit no kids or some nigga or whatever and that was exciting, like, that made me excited for you, because it meant you could be like that too."

"Boy please, I do have my own hobbies and life and shit."

"Okay, like what?" I said. "What's a thing you do that don't have nothin to do with us or gettin out from under some nigga?"

"Well, you know...Joey shit," she rolled her eyes. "It don't matter."

"Yes it do."

"No it don't."

"Yes it do."

"Joey stop playin wit me."

"Yes it do."

She started ticklin me while I was driving. "Chill!" I said. "Chill, damn."

"You chill."

"This that kinda shit niggas who don't know how to drive do. You still not tryna learn how to drive?"

"No. My man can—"

"Please don't say that shit. Please don't say it."

"What Joey? I got plenty of niggas out here that'll drive me where I gotta be. Fuckin ask about me."

"Like me, huh."

"Shut up."

We was stuck in traffic then on I-95. She was eatin Andy Capp's Hot Fries and lookin a little too hard at the banana Otis on my dash.

"Don't you wanna get married?" she said.

"Fuck no," I said. "I already got too many jobs."

"Joey everything ain't no damn job."

"It is if you want a safe place to live."

"Boy."

"What?"

"You do not know everything like you think you know."

"What I don't know then?"

"Everything."

"Like what?"

"You lonely."

"Who the fuck ain't. Ain't you lonely?"

"No, I got plenty of people."

"Where they at?"

She grunted. Then she pulled out a cigarette. "Can I smoke one of—"

"Girl hell no you can't smoke in my car, that shit stink and we all got asthma. Even my kids."

"God Joey it ain't even that deep."

"Well if you learn how to drive you can have your own car and smoke that shit up."

She said nothing at first. "What happened to that tall girl you used to mess wit? I liked her."

"That was the least specific shit I ever heard in my life. The rapper?"

"No not her, that was years ago. You know who I'm talkin about."

"No I don't."

"Yes you do."

"No I don't."

"Her name begin wit a *L* I think but it was weird."

"Oh! Yeah, we gettin married."

She stared at me. "You play too much."

"She dumped me cause I was too distant and then we got back together and I told her regular shit that she wasn't tryna hear or deal wit then I dumped her out of resentment and she had an abortion and now we work together, kinda, but still friends."

"You was bout to have another baby? God damn, boy!"

"Are you really talkin right now? And no, not technically, the dad coulda been this other dude too."

She laughed. "I only got three." Then she tried to pull the cigarette out again.

"No!" I said.

"Shit Joey you so annoying, get on my nerves. Why yall don't get back together?"

"Why would we just 'get back together'? It don't even work like that."

"You swear you know how everything work."

"Says the person who just asked me how to eat pussy."

"You would like my new girlfriend. She's great."

"I doubt it."

"What?"

"Nothing. You talk to Mika?"

"She still not talkin to me."

"She not talkin to you or you not talkin to her?"

"She not talkin to me."

"Because you not talkin to her?"

"No because she not talkin to me."

"What if it's because you not talkin to her?"

"She attacked me, Joey."

"What if it's because she feel like you be attackin her?"

"She crazy."

"You know how that sound coming from you, right?"

"She crazier than me."

"You know what's crazy?"

"What?"

"That you keep tryna take them cigarettes out in my car."

"But Joeeeey," she whined. "I need one."

"I need a million dollars."

"Well you got them jobs, you on your way, lemme have a goddamn cigarette."

"Absofuckinglutely not, unless you tryna walk to the PO."

"It's not that deep, just one."

"No."

She shook her head and cracked the window. Lit a cigarette. "Ain't nobody bout to tell me what the fuck I'm bout to do out here I'm a grown ass woman, don't know who the fuck he think he is little nigga don't know everything," she mumbled.

I gave her the book *She Comes First*, which I'd never read and had originally gotten from Ray back in the day. She never read the text nor ate her girlfriend's pussy, she told me, because the girl started beating on her. "These girls out here actin just like the men now," she said.

Her PO was a brown-skin woman in her thirties who'd gone to public school in Philly too, and so there were things she knew. She was gentle at first, laying out the regimen my mother would need to adhere to. Where I needed to take her and when: the NA meetings and job hunts, the therapy sessions and doctor's appointments, all the medications and triggers and not a single release valve. It was easy to let my eyes relax and glaze over when she spoke, and I said I would review her notes though there were honestly too many; it might have been easier to collate diagnoses in the negative, to ask what wasn't wrong and build a shorter list: schizophrenia, bipolar disorder, drug abuse disorder, complex PTSD, violent outbursts and on and on and on and on and on and my mother, next to me, was playing *Candy Crush* and texting her geriatric boyfriend, this white guy in the Northeast whom she'd later ask me to kill.

In therapy she seemed closed off, my mother; whenever the therapist recounted an experience and asked her how she felt about it she was all "It is what it is. You know," and "How much longer we got left?" Her affect was flat except when *I* was asked questions, surprised, for reasons I could never understand, that I was so open to discussion in unsentimental transparency on topics as diverse as sex and stealing or her friend's fingers in my nine-year-old anus while fellating me; I was then already so bored with the pretense of some endemic otherwise, and the social and literary demands of suspending one's disbelief concerning reality: the obvious fact that the world can be trying and bad things can happen, especially to children and those occupying the lower rungs of a continually shifting classarchy up to and including the identitarian categories that appear in popular discourse as overdeterminations which wide swaths of people with very little or too much power both love a great deal, because they afford recognition without thought or feeling, and give us nap time next to abstractions like freedom, ultimately absconding from the recognition that being treated poorly makes us more, rather than less, common. She must have blocked out my being molested by her friends or that I told her without much fanfare about PTSD or being dubbed bipolar too, the times I'd tried to kill myself; these were old things that everyone we knew dealt with, and so I could not understand how it broke her down. And to be honest, I was angry at her willingness to make it about me, though only in ways that excused doing the work, as if tenderness or tears alone might rescue us.

"Mom," I kept saying. "Mom. Look. I'm gonna be fine. Look."

She cried into her hands. "I'm so sorry Joey. I'm so sorry I failed. I don't know what to do."

This was perhaps the only time she'd been asked to do nothing, except for herself; the terms of inevitable failure, or the insane American idea that this failure could somehow be *her* fault, were not interesting to me.

Though she was right before, I was lonely. So lonely that what I wanted most of all was for her to quit the attempts to care for me and the claims of regret, so that we could be less so, together: regretful, and lonely. Had she the independence to bear a friendship with me that she seemed to want, we might both survive. But the scripts of family that have long since failed to serve us were too important to her still. Embarrassed, and unable to use language in a way that made sense, I'd cry too. For hours we'd sit there, then on our way back home in tears we'd pretend that something might come out of it, but it never did.

My mother needed things, either from me or other men. She needed money. When I got her a job at the hospital, she quit the first week because she didn't wanna wake up at seven, then she asked me to buy her the new iPhone. When I said no, she threw a tantrum. "Fuck you then Joey!" she said. "I don't gotta deal with this shit, fuck you!" She left her dirty bras and panties all over my bathroom. She left food out overnight and attracted bugs. She broke televisions, remotes and ceiling fans, destroyed wallpaper and drank all the wine and beer, smashed the glasses and plates clumsily, ate all the food I cooked for her, leaving none for me or the kids and set off smoke alarms whenever she tried to make her own; she promised to help around the house and slept on the living room couch screaming if kids made noise getting ready for school; she stayed up all night yelling on the phone or smoking inside and had men come to pick her up at all hours of the night, waking the kids and telling them to shut the fuck up if they cried. I tried and cried and repeated, stored up energy to lead conversations with her that I would never bother having with anyone else on any given day after work.

Cleaning up dirty panties from the bathroom I'd ask her, "Mom, can you double-check after you shower to make sure you got the clothes up?"

"Oh whatever Joey I gave birth to you the least you could do is pick up some fuckin clothes, damn."

With no more food I'd beckon, "Mom that was all we had left. Can you just let me know you need something to eat before you go in?"

When she screamed and cursed the kids I'd tell her, "Mom you gotta chill out a little bit they not tryna bother you they babies and talkin to them like that ain't gonna help anyway."

This went on for years. Till the day I saw her slap my son and call him a fucking sissy for dancing in the living room in his sister's *Frozen* Halloween costume singing "Let It Go."

From then on I'd remained her emergency contact, picking her up from hospitals after overdoses, dragging her to and from rehabs, sending her money for food, threatening her boyfriends and breaking up their fights, bringing her home from Lancaster or Valley Forge or Croyden or wherever she got stuck, missing work, dates, my own appointments for mental health, courtroom battles. I tried to move forward at her pace: establishing boundaries or asking safe questions, suggesting rather than telling her what she might do, being clear about what I could offer, the how and why. But it only got worse. My credit was maxed and she'd trashed the apartments rented in my name, would show up at my place looking for beer and breaking in if I wasn't home, ripping through the petproof screen for some reason and leaving with bottles of wine and hot Cheetos, packs of ramen and frozen chicken. When I told her to stay away, her expression didn't change and she finally accepted for the first time ever, that she no longer had anyone, I felt, to love her.

And so it never made sense to me, the idea of representing or uplifting a race when I couldn't even do this for my own mother. So no, I was not proud of myself for anything, of the platitudes or celebrations, of how the hospitals or the prisons or me or my siblings treated her, or the way said treatment was described for an audience, of not describing said treatment for an audience, of how she would be located in the founding doctrines of the world as a magical creature instead of a human being, the center of all our collective failings both real and imaginary. And so I think I died then, a little, at the loss of certain futures together, she and I, me and her, being a parent, being parented, being a people, being a happy people. Alive.

—

ASLEEP, MY MOTHER SEEMS kinder, and just short of beautiful. I consider the kinds of pleasures she might want access to in another life. She snores. And I'm back to chronicling the parable of our lives, to her chagrin. My guilt is useless, and I ask myself were my father a woman would I have taken him seriously, would I have tried with him? Expended the time and energy and resources and failed care? My mother's blood pressure is low, but it's always been too low when she's hooked and thin. Every time in her chart, something new. Cash App requests on my phone. I thought this cost $1,500.00 but it actually costs $1,900.00. Send me the money now. Are you going to take them YES or NO? I will be documenting this for my attorney but I am invested in your healing and me and the children will be here when you decide to change your behaviors. What did you do with my wife? Just tell me what you did. Did the dog scratch him? I will have photographs for the next hearing. I linger on the newest Belize swimsuit options. The last thirteen voice mails are all from Ray, hard to hear, or my mother, spiraling. *Come pick me up right now! I'm out West. These niggas think I'm playin, they don't know the truth though. Joey I don't give a fuck where you at I told you to come get me right now, shit Joey damn. Is your sister okay? Joey are you still messin wit that girl that used to be a boy? Joey come get me what the fuck I'm at Plymouth Meeting I think. No. It's like Neshaminy, the other one I'm right in front of the movies. Joey lemme get some money. I only need like a hundred dollars I'll get it back to you. Joey pick up the fuckin phone it's your mother!*

My mother wakes up groggy and says something inconceivable about love. She's embarrassed and angry. "Joey why the fuck they got these things on me again, take this shit off me!" she says. "Can't stand this shit yall don't know who you fuckin wit fuckin wit me imma show yall."

"You was bitin people."

She calms a bit at this, remembering. "So what," she says then. "I don't give a fuck they shouldnta put no hands on me I don't give a fuck bout none of that take these damn restraints off me."

I take her right hand out and give her some water, jotting it in my notes on the computer. "You know how this goes," I say. "They not gonna let you leave till you sober and chill."

"Joey, chill my ass, these people don't got no say over me." She takes a sip of water.

"Don't look that way," I say. "I can't just break you out. You was in the middle of the boulevard midtraffic wilin out, cussing, screaming, making threats. The ambulance had to wrestle you out the street. No shirt on."

"I called you," she says.

"Yes Mom you always call me and I can't do it every time I'm fuckin tired and I'm at work."

"And," she says, "so am I." She sips some more water

and starts nodding off. "Always at work. Work not no excuse to keep neglecting ya family Joey."

And in this, she sounds like Myra, who hates the fact of my working almost as much as my not having enough money. On the computer I recognize that I'd forgotten to pay for QueenWolf9k's school trip and her new glasses, which I'm told are ready. GodRex96's trip is soon too, where I'd volunteered to chaperone and only now realize it's on one of the days I was supposed to be in Belize. I need to buy a new twin mattress and couch too, both too thoroughly pissed on. There aren't anymore groceries; the fridge is empty. I didn't save enough money for all the summer camps, and early enrollment is soon if I want to secure them all spots. I extend my shift a couple more hours.

MOM HAD GOT LOCKED up a bunch of times, most prominently for drug possession, prostitution, and then assault; if I remember right, she was away for two straight years at the longest, always in and out, cycling through short sentences and rehab programs but in this particular moment my brother's ex had taken over her mantle and has not, as of yet, accepted any phone calls. My sister hasn't been locked up yet, but by the time I came back home, her boyfriend, with whose kid she was pregnant, would soon pistol-whip her and do his time for assault and possession after running around the city feigning fear that either I or my grandfather would shoot him. My friend Trey was locked up for like eleven years and ended up workin at Home Depot with me back in the day and does contracting now; we play ball on Sunday mornings too. Popop was locked up for attempted murder, but never talks about it other than an acquiescence to "stupid gang shit." Ganny had been locked up a bunch for the same things as her daughter, the same things as her mother before. My dad, apparently, had been locked up for everything. I hadn't been locked up yet because after grabbing another job as a transport EMT on the weekends I was almost up to date on child support and, luckily, the last time my mom asked me to kill her boyfriend for beating her the cops arrived first and let me take her away, bloody and sweaty and having pissed herself, so she could sober up. Her boyfriend died the next day. A heart attack. A while after that I sold my gun cause I was broke anyway, and figured it was too big a risk; and now I'd left it in my locker after buying it back on sale, circling the same narrow call-and-response back home.

For as long as I can remember I've had nightmares about prison. Being there, always. The jailhouse loomed large in my imagination; I dreamed it was inescapable, and once, a black therapist called this premonition and we talked about which positions we might take in the Baldwin story "Going to Meet the Man," how the subconscious might be all about sex yes Freud, but also, depending on your subject position, prison. It was our most familiar locale. An inverse to the college I attend in the other Philadelphia. My mother had given birth to me there in the prison, while visiting some man not my father. And I could still recall the visits to men who were sweet to me from behind the glass, men who needed my mother to bring them things they could sell. Men who died there. My mother's brothers, her dad and them. Their faces are mostly indistinguishable at this point, though my feelings seemed to be intensifying alongside my own material distance from them. And maybe this is why I've neglected visiting my dad before knowing anything about him, why when my clearances come through so does the urge to abandon the project altogether, why I've neglected entering any prison as an adult and eschewed the many inside-out programs I'd been invited to, why even now, when my dad comes into the hospital half-conscious, I hesitate moving toward him like it's not my job.

—

AND HERE HE IS, stuck and arguably stable. They got him lying flat on this stretcher with ripped sheets and his tiny right hand with the rose tattoo attached to the long side rail. He slides the cuffed hand up past the top of his dome and down to his white Air Forces, stretching his shoulder, or advancing a form of curiosity that does, like my brother had said, make him seem childish. The guards are bored, one this new white guy sitting too close to Rell's free hand and the other standing up, inches from the TV flicking through channels with increasing disappointment.

"You the nurse?" the guard says. And even though I've seen this boul too many times for my soul he still asks this and I tell him naw, while linking Rell up to the monitor. "Imma go over to the bathroom real quick then," he says, dropping the remote on Rell's chest the way most facilitators organize patient care objects and cell phones, mouthwash, toothpaste and new pillows, the bloody towels after cleaning a wound.

Rell is hardly with it, but obviously in pain. His feet look massacred: cuts, wounds, scabs, holes, pus and missing chunks leaking into the foot of the stretcher and smelling as they do. Obvious there's hardly treated diabetes but this is much more than that, and since this is the hospital, where the extraction of such informa-tion is standard and necessary, I slip into inquiry same as I always do with new patients.

"What's up man?" I say. "I'm Joseph and imma be workin wit your nurse, what's going on today?"

He looks up at me slow but not the least bit curi-ous and tells me, "You know what, young boul, that's interesting cause I got a son with that name." But other than this he doesn't move. "You know," he goes on. "So they told me about this Johnson & Johnson study. Ath-lete's foot treatment, you know I always had real bad feet and this jawn was payin like $50.00. You just had to try the powder to see if it helped but that shit start eatin away at me man. I kept it going cause at first I thought how sometimes shit be burnin when it's sposed to work, like if it don't hurt at least a little bit it ain't doin nothin anyway but it wouldn't never stop. That shit never stopped."

Assessing the wounds, his explanation seems like an understatement. When I lift his feet—painful to the touch—they feel like hollow air wrapped in skin, the texture of which, even through my gloves, is how I imagine the folds of Freddy Krueger's cheeks might feel. This is not quite like a burn victim, of whom I've touched many, after fires and years later, explosions, their flesh sheared off in a matter of seconds; Rell's predicament feels more like the steady erosion of wear and tear, without the wear or clear-eyed comprehension of its prominence. I'm startled but don't show it, at the maggots wriggling beneath the skin, tight nodules that make me wonder how he walks on these feet at all. The rookie guarding him looks over in disgust, pinching his nose.

"I dare you to eat it," he says.

Rell doesn't respond to this, accustomed or plain flaccid to humiliation. He goes on to explain the ins and outs of this particular study and how much more it pays by comparison; he was tired of working the kitchen for shit, cleaning showers and toilets "like a fuckin slave" and seeing no way out. The studies were a way for him to participate in the world, to interact with, at the very least, something like an outside he might not otherwise ever touch again. If it worked, he would be helping people, and this idea really kept him going. I think in this moment of how often folks from Holmesburg or other State Road haunts come back, how, despite the force of injury and how it might be exacerbated by the care they receive here, they always seemed glad for the sounds and the air, for the car ride and stretcher with its adjustable head. I'm also overwhelmed by the man's dullness. Besides the symbolic force of mythology nothing stands out. Except of course the ears, like looking into a mirror: the old joke of selfsame physiognomy come home to roost. This feels just as irrelevant as not, and more boring than I can admit to myself in the moment.

And so he wants apple juice, like everybody and they mom. By the time he asks I'm no longer wondering if he'll recognize me, but why would he? The length of my imagination suggests that he might have other concerns, only one of which I'm in a position to certify. Of the few remaining apple juices in those tiny plastic cups with aluminum lids, two are open. This is especially odd since they hardly sit stable on the frigerator racks and maybe I'm moving too slowly, sliding the half-drunk ones out of the way, both in denial about the fact that it's past time to head upstairs, knowing I should have already been there, or my refusal to consider the fact that Ray is dead, that I've known he was dead since the moment I saw what was left of him slide into the trauma bay. I've known he was dead the same way I've always known how most of us will be maimed or killed in easily

measurable order. I'm lilting, and a bit dizzy, considering an apple juice myself now or anything else scaveng-
able in the vicinity, and Uma sees this but doesn't say
anything, just points at the white tub in front of her and
come-hithers me.

More often than not, the products of conception,
as they are now, keep sealed in a white tub just larger
than my hand by the nurse's station, having grown cold
alone for hours to the repulsion of its too-human family.
There were arguments, nurses screaming at each other
about how someone could leave the aborted baby in a
big white jar on the counter for everyone to see; no one
wanted to touch it; no one ever wants to touch it, and
even the requests for its removal are tepid or pleading.
*Could you please take...this thing downstairs to the lab?* Or *If
you're able, I know this is delicate, but I won't ask you for anything else if you can get this to the lab for me.* People hold the
bucket as if renaming "products of conception" hadn't
already solved the problem, as if it will bite them; they
nudge it out of view as they sit, seal it with tape sometimes, write euphemisms on the outside to ensure no
one opens it, whole time, of course, of course, the patient
whose body from whence it came sits across the room
behind a thin curtain listening to the drama unfold,
hearing how put off the whole floor has become at their
loss. That I don't wear gloves when grabbing it elicits
gasps and gagging too loud for anyone not to hear.

Downstairs by the lab the morgue door no longer closes, and there are children running in and out,
some staring at the cold tub in my hand and making
faces. Some thawing and others creeping around with
their phones out, hunting for Pokémon. I drop off the
products of conception and join them in *Pokémon Go! Of
course*, I think *of course* this is the perfect place for ghosts.
Gengars and Haunters and Drifblim make space out of
place, time out of incontinuity here. One of the children
asks what my favorite Pokémon is and I tell her Drago-
nite; hers is Flaaffy, which makes me laugh.

"Ain't no Flaaffy down here though," I say.

"How you know?" she says. "Just cause you can't
find none?" Then she walks off, to find some Flaaffy.

Her friends are in the morgue giggling, gently lift-
ing sheets or unzipping bags to peer into the faces of
the dead. Normally, I'd tell them to get the fuck outta
there and go find their parents. They glide their little
hands across the bodies, curious. Most of them hardly
notice me. One climbs under a sheet, on top of a body,
making ghost sounds and they laugh and laugh until I
hear someone running down the stairs to retrieve me.

"Joseph hurry up! We need more hands," Rasheeda
says, sweating.

Upstairs looks a bit more chaotic than normal,
folks running around in loops, crisscrossing in the hallway, through the nurse's station and in and out of the
trauma bay. An Amtrak train, it turns out, derailed,

sending dozens of patients our way at a time. The nurse manager upstairs is aware it'll be a while now; she even sends more hands down to help. Going from zero to a hundred for several blank hours I swim through the crowd of bodies in practiced repetition.

No one dies.

I STAND UP ON THE opposite side of the nurse's station, too tired to sit and ever get back up, shifting between writing and scanning through patient names and ailments, triaging them in my head in order to decide who to grab from the waiting room, who needs to be looked in on, and who would inevitably need some procedure or test that I, in my capacity as an ED tech, could start now rather than having them sit a few hours in unnecessary silence or screaming. It's a struggle to catch up after the Amtrak; the chief complaints are mostly recognizable: 75 y/o woman with leg pain, 16 y/o male with urinary problems, two families' worth of minor car accidents, a 33 y/o man (who I've known for years) with sickle cell problems, three different assaults, six chest pains, some mild anaphylaxis, a few low-grade fevers and at the very bottom a man named Frederick Douglass with a blank chief complaint section—only thing listed is a comment, which isn't linked to a particular user in the electronic medical records system. It says, as though unveiling a deeper truth: "Chief Complaint: Escaped from slavery."

I'm crackin the fuck up, until a wave of nausea hits. A white physician with whom on various occasions I'd exchanged oral sex is laughing in a way that I'm sure they think is with me, and way too hard. *Was it that funny? Did this setting, from a particular vantage point, make it funnier?* Everyone seems to be in on the joke, seems to have glanced at the EMR simultaneously. Is the escape itself viable as a chief complaint, or is this a weird reification obscuring, or revealing, a set of material problems? And to what extent are the best jokes doing so? Why did someone in the late-twentieth-century name their child Frederick Douglass, and why, like the many schools named after MLK, did this person have to be so sickly and so dying and so bereft in this place hundreds of years later, in this position? And how many times has he been to prison? Four times, it turns out, though for mostly nonviolent offenses, the likes of which liberals can easily fold into redemptive gesture; in other words, he might be salvageable.

DOUGLASS'S ACTUAL COMPLAINTS ARE numerous, as much so as any older black person in North Philly. He has high blood pressure and heart problems, diabetes that had taken a few toes, a stent put in however long ago, some vague note written as "gum problems," is prone to seizures, has had one stroke so far, and he'd been shot on three different occasions. And yet, somehow, here he is, walking into room 13 on his own two feet with little guidance, an ambivalent, zombie-like gesture that I'm not exactly looking forward to. He looks, above all, tired. This time, he's here for a psych problem; there is always a psych problem, either real or manufactured by the real. It surprises me that we're not all here for psych problems. Either way, I wonder how, in this many visits to the ED, I've never met him till now.

There's no sheet on the stretcher in room 13 but Douglass sits down on the bed anyway, then lies down, fully supine in silence. His fro balls up under the back of his head and he puts a black power pick down on the bedside table, staring up at the popcorn ceiling like it might eat him. I'd seen in his notes that he would be on 1:1 observation—sitting and watching within arm's reach—a task that often falls to ED techs, as I had just sat with my mother. This happens so often that too often, there is a lack of clarity about exactly why someone is on a 1:1. They just are. Psych problem. The reason they need to be guarded, imprisoned, and restrained if necessary is of little importance compared to the fact that they need to be guarded, imprisoned or restrained immediately. "Psych problem" covers a whole range of psychological differences, or emotional dispensations ranging from telling a physician no or not knowing who the president is upon cognitive exam (most people don't), to bipolar disorder, drug overdose or good old-fashioned threats of interpersonal violence. *Escaped from slavery*, I suppose, was also historically manufactured as a psych problem. A few weeks ago, this other patient on a 1:1 broke a nurse's jaw when she tried to take his blood pressure, then he crushed the ED tech under the stretcher and ran outta the room until security tackled and cuffed him, putting him in full body restraints. Said patient had been chill just a moment prior.

Douglass is silent.

"Hey man, how you doin?" I say. "I'm Joseph, I'm gonna be sittin with you for safety today."

Douglass keeps staring up at the ceiling. Doesn't say a word. Then he turns to me real slow. "Call me Fred," he says. "I done heard all this shit before man."

I'm not sure what "all this shit" means for him specifically, only generally, so in my head I make the adjustment and call it clear. I ask him if I can check his vitals, you know, standard procedure, and instead of responding he puts his arm out, bored already with the routine. You can always tell how many times somebody's been around by how their body acclimates to the field of power. When the cuff inflates, Fred is crying. First low, and then full-blown sobs and wailing.

"Hey man," I say, my hand on his shoulder. "Is there anything I can do?"

"No," he says. "No…I'm so sorry. I don't know what's wrong anymore."

D COMES BY THEN. Soon as I start to settle in at a portable computer, documenting Fred's disposition and reading the email about the note attached to his chart, the culprit, one of my favorite physicians, among the few black ones, is fired for the joke. Having waited for Fred to fall asleep, D swings through the curtain saying there's a trauma coming. There's always a trauma coming. I've started to think, at this point, that the only form of recognition in life is trauma. D is always hunting for 1:1 opportunities so he can sit down and play *Final Fantasy Tactics* while some patient is nodding off or cussing him out through restraints. We've all just kinda acquiesced to it. And here he was throwing me outta the room to go do some chest compressions and get bled on so he could hang with drugged-up-sleeping Fred and luxuriate on the rolling hospital chair behind a curtain where, ostensibly, he was winning *The War of the Lions*.

"You ain't hear it?" he says. "You must be deaf, nigga, all them bombs." And I'm reminded that he and I are also two of five folks here who'd been deployed to

Iraq or Afghanistan in the past couple years, and that we shared a trepidation regarding loud noises for some time, till the hospital beat it out of us.

I just half roll my eyes at him; I am, technically, the one assigned to trauma. "Aight man," I say. "You hear what it was?"

"Explosion is all I got," he pulls out a Twizzler, half-chewed. "But I took the last two, so let me switch wit you and you come back after this one."

"Aight, cool," I say, getting up. "Lemme log off." He gives me a Twizzler and I eat it on my way out.

IN THE TRAUMA BAY everybody is sharing sour candy and Skittles and broken-off Otis bits and cafeteria bacon under pure white hyperartificial lights; it's always bright like an autopsy room, which half the time it is. There's another Otis Spunkmeyer muffin on the crash cart, unopened but blueberry, so it might as well be trash. My favorite night nurse, Mona, is here. She hasn't been nursing long, only a few years, and both of us are still surprised sometimes at how many people can work in such a small space simultaneously: arms weaving in and out and over other arms and heads and hands and legs intertwined, with sneakers on top of clogs and needles and scopes and digits all clawing at a single, naked, hapless body. Whenever I walk past her, she pinches my ass, but neither of us seem sure. She refers to all whites as snow honkeys out loud; no one says anything. She's short and goofy and does CrossFit and those morning workouts at the art museum with Rasheeda too and you can find her between patients reading *Drinking Coffee Elsewhere* at the charge desk. She's also married to this black British respiratory therapist lady who is very nice but whose accent I cannot stand and works per diem at every other hospital in Philly.

There are three new residents waiting excitedly, or terrified; sometimes it's hard to tell the difference, or they all look the same. The whole trauma team, invested in the potential gore, seething, perhaps, from Amtrak's infliction of only minor wounds, are all shoved into the corner cooing in front of a computer screen at some person's broken or disfigured or torn-off or blown-off something or other. One of the residents, a short black dude whose name we always forget or neglect to remember outta sheer pettiness, in part, because he hardly remembers ours, says, "They're coming from I-676, that's like twenty minutes away at least." I always feel like he code-switches a little too much and wears those too-big cubic zirconia earrings, like Ludacris on a budget, or maybe it's because he always seems the most nervous, I dunno, that baby afro length that can't decide whether it wants to be a low-cut Caesar or transcend into the cornrows of futures past, but something is really preventing me from liking him. He stands at the head of the stretcher, ostensibly to work the airway, strangling the neck of a laryngoscope in his right hand like a lover, but only after they've begged him to do so and he returns to his friends big sad about how finding a lover is hard because, as a black man, women only want him to hurt them, explaining that his natural disposition is actually, in contradistinction to stereotypes, more kind and gentle. He's just too gentle for fucking and wants to make love. That Tierra prefers being choked from behind seemed at first odd to me, because I too was once a child.

For a minute everyone sits in silence, some suckling and chewing Sour Patch Kids with the vigor of starving ruminants. And I'm thinking, *Don't it hurt to chew like that?* My mother chews like that sometimes and I can't stand it, my mother who still has not been discharged and for whom I'd just brought in some doughnuts and coffee, three slices of bacon, an over-easy egg, lightly toasted hash browns and Tropicana orange juice and who yelled, while eating it, that it was nasty and not enough, about how I didn't pay attention to what she asked. I walked out. Of the three stretchers in the room, two are unoccupied and the flock of scrubs huddle around the middle one, checking watches, examining equipment. In the first bed there's a drunk HIV+ octogenarian man who falls a lot in leather restraints until he sobers up enough to go home. Mona's friend

Jessica is leaning on the bed with one elbow, pointing at people and assigning them duties with the other hand: IV, vitals, clothes, family, IV, blood bank, etc. When she's done, Anya, the attending physician, starts playing music through her phone, beginning with Pink, "Sober," exercising an obsession with songs naming or involving sobriety which make you want to drink or do harder drugs.

"Who the hell gets blown up on 676 anyway?" Rasheeda says. "It's sweet as shit over there."

"I don't even understand what that means," I say. *Blown up?*

"Maybe it was a drone strike," Mona whispers to me.

Is it a child? I laugh anyway. She takes a deep breath, already drenched in sweat beneath her plastic gown. Then she rips it off. "Well I'm not wearing this shit for twenty more minutes."

I whisper back to her, "You know I coulda done that, right?"

She hits me on my side, then puts her arm around my waist to pull me closer. Jessica rolls the fuck outta her eyes.

"And I'm gonna go pee then," another resident, Schneider, jumps in. "I always gotta pee after I put all this shit on." He starts removing the protective lead, a face shield, plastic gown, sterile gloves, the footies over his clogs and all. But just as Schneider opens the door to walk out, three medics rush into the trauma bay. One on the trauma's chest, or what's left of it, one bagging, and another sort of steering.

Earl—biceps tearing through a medium blue fire rescue shirt like always—moves the trauma from one stretcher to another by himself, saying, "Twenty-three-year-old male, explosion. Family said they always knew this would happen."

"This is why you don't play with guns, kids," Jessica says.

"What?" I say.

"You can't hear, nigga?" D says. He comes outta nowhere, having been relieved by a psych tech from upstairs.

"Help me with the clothes," Rasheeda says.

Mona takes over compressions first, but D slides Mona aside and makes the stretcher squeal with every depression. Shears come out and clothes come off. Mona hooks the trauma up to a monitor and starts a line in his left arm without a thought. That resident is still clutching the laryngoscope, staring at the ET tube already hanging from the patient's mouth.

"You can put that down now man," Jessica says, conducting people with the patience of an elementary school teacher. The attending directs that resident to speak with the family, all of whom we hear yelling and screaming and weeping at security just outside. Anya takes charge. Other doctors watch, scrutinizing. I switch off with D and it feels like squelching into

Jell-O. Epinephrine. Vasopressin. Atropine. Repeat. The trauma has already had two thousand liters of fluid and no pulse. Chunks of metal hang out of his body like *Tetsuo*. Schneider orders blood. I switch off with D again to fetch blood from the lab downstairs, glancing at the children still playing *Pokémon Go!* by the morgue, then running back up and handing it off to Mona who, looking down at the trauma, but seeing no reason to do so, spikes the blood as ordered.

The trauma looks both younger and older than twenty-three. Blood and spinal fluid coagulating into the sheet of the stretcher, flesh mostly bare and prodded. Both me and Mona draw stethoscopes to get manual BPs, her careening her neck and body to avoid the brain matter plopping to the floor and making space for Anya's main resident to wedge in between her and the trauma with a portable echocardiogram, and me ducking under Jessica and another nurse on a stool and feeling someone's tired elbow resting on my shoulder. Fully extending her arms, Mona places the bell end of her stethoscope over the trauma's brachial artery; nothing. I hear nothing on the other side. Schneider sploshes around on the trauma's gelled chest with a probe. Another nurse straightens out the trauma's left arm for a third IV after the second comes out; there's a cracking sound; he fails once, then gets a flash.

We're obviously at a dead end, but it's good practice at a teaching hospital. Mona and I just look at each other, slowing down. Jessica looks like she's about to sit; she diverts her energy to flirting with the other medic, Rodge, who she used to fuck before she got pregnant by one of the residents. Anya is yawning, lookin at her phone. The lull gives me time to make faces at Mona and not look away when she looks back. I'm reminded of way back when, during my first week of training when I was still struggling to remember the supply room code, just bleep-bleeping at the buttons on the door for like eight minutes while someone was dying until Mona came up behind me, reached around and unlocked the door without looking at the numbers. When we got in there, I felt rushed to grab IV tubing but couldn't find it. When I asked if she could help she pushed up against me and I backed up kind of instinctively as she climbed onto a stool, then reached over my head to grab the tubing.

"Duh," she said a couple inches from my face.

She smiled, went back flat on her feet and walked outta the storeroom. That was only my third time or so talking to her, notwithstanding a barrage of too-intimate questions at lunch with a bunch of other people walking in and out of the break room. That patient died.

Mona tells Jessica to stop being a fat pregnant hoe and connects another bag of fluids, staring at Anya as she does. Anya gives Mona that look, like, *What*? Three rounds of chest compressions, epinephrine, ventilations and suction later, the trauma's heart is officially still.

Anya finally says, "Okay, okay, anyone want to call it? He's leaking CSF, most of his brain is gone and the heart has yet to move." She's calm, smooth and just loud enough for everyone to hear her. She stands near the entrance of the trauma bay in an unweathered white coat with crisp maroon scrubs underneath.

"Time of death, 18:53," Schneider says, dropping the probe where he stands. Its cord catches on the stretcher's rail, dangling just before hitting the ground.

Jessica pats him on the shoulder. "You did good, man."

All the residents and the respiratory therapist, the attending and most of the nurses too, clear out of the bay so we can clean. Total time: nine minutes.

Once they're gone, D starts singing, "Another one bites the dust." He makes a gesture of a gun with his fingers on the trauma's left temple.

"You ain't even right," Mona says.

"If loving you is wrong," D says, saddling up beside her, hand around her waist. "I don't wanna—"

"Boy get off me," Mona says, laughing and pushing him off.

"See that tattoo," says another nurse, pointing at the trauma. "He must be military."

"Great," says D. "What a jackass. Now this'll be added to some statistic about military suicides." He flails his arms. "Those crazy fuckers with the PTSD again. He prolly never even fuckin deployed."

There's a brightly colored Semper Fi Marine Corps eagle tattoo on the new trauma's left bicep. It's peppered with a few drops of blood, but otherwise clean and well done. Recent. The nurses and techs separate his belongings, each item to its own brown paper bag.

THE WHOLE SIXTH FLOOR smells like shit; it's a *C. diff* kind of day, one of those ultra-instinct smells almost as hard to articulate as the crack your grandparents are smoking in your bathroom when you come home and everybody otherwise tries to act normal. Lise stays for some extra hours to start training an overnight person and Shay picks up our kids, texting both of us in a group chat I can't stand neither one of you niggas I'm supposed to be on vacation and I got everybody kids yall all at work being lovey dovey and shit you niggas owe and these kids might not even make it through the day they better not try to play me. Lise and I both Cash App $250.00 for the time and expense. While I'm at it, I send my mother another $25.00 for cigarettes to stop the texts and calling since they've taken off her restraints and Your Aunt Suzie never woke up after she had the baby; I send my sister $532.00 because she needs new tires after another boyfriend, still stalking her, shreds all four of hers Thank you bro I don't know what I would do without you; I send $300.00 to Cee because he'd overdrawn his account by accident, but I'll get that back in about a week. Did you know Rome got locked up again, that's why he wasn't hoopin last Sunday. My account is overdrawn now, but only by $132.00 with the max being $600.00 gives a little wiggle room, and I have my credit card available for the next few days until the paycheck comes, and then what I'll make back from all this overtime. I see an additional shift open on the computer and bid for that too. There are four call bells going off: One is a patient whose face I recognize from those back-to-school drives where they hand out free book bags in front of the church in Germantown; they want Rice Krispies Treats, which I can't find; another is my great-grandmother who, when I walk into the room, says, "Joey? How long, bout how long, I know they told me I forget how long you been workin here?" My great-grandmother, appearing health-ier than her sons numbers-wise but who will also soon die from breast cancer, has questions. "How all them kids doin?" she says.

QueenWolf9k has started to inquire about my sex life. How do you have sex with a girl, versus how you have sex with a boy? How did you and Mommy used to have sex? What does it feel like? I tell her that things were once glorious, sex being a big part—I don't say the only part—of our relationship, her mother and

I. Your mother and I waited until you finally went to sleep, or other times while you were watching TV or playing *LEGO Jurassic World,* she loved to climb on top of me to cum, to such an extent that as I got older, I would sprain muscles if I did not drink enough water or stretch. She returns to *It's Perfectly Normal* in preparation for more questions, then looks back at me and decidedly admits that yes, I am old, and that she doesn't know if she likes girls or boys yet and, even though this is interesting, she's not ready for sex yet either. I tell her that's great and that she can come holler at me when she wants to talk more, which will inevitably be the next night wherein she will have finally gathered the courage to ask about the bougie fleshlight sitting on my bathroom sink after I catch her playing with it, having the whole thing inside out and repeating to herself, *This is weird, this is soooo weird.* We'd beef that night when, a few hours into a heated game of *Naruto Monopoly,* me laughing after she'd hit the "straight to jail" spot twice in a row and then went bankrupt after landing on my Hidden Leaf Village with two hotels, my hand out like "Pay up, pay up" and reminding her of the all too confident "Where my rent at Father?" two turns earlier and realizing, after slowly counting her colored bills, that she could not make it in Konoha, she screamed, slamming the money down on the table and crashing into her room, slamming the door behind her. "Good game!" I yelled from the living room.

GodRaptor69, having taken to calling his brothers idiots and telling my sister to suck his dick whenever she asks him to do something, now asks every day if I can take him to Target for toys. Confused about this, I'm always like no, why would I do that and he responds, flat as ever, that this is why he loves Mommy more: Not only does she have cupcakes, but she will also take him to Target for toys. I tell him to please be quiet and eat the motherfuckin roasted broccoli before he never sees a toy again in his life. He cries for over an hour, sulking while the others stare on in amusement, until BumblebeeFort slides in and eats the broccoli in exchange for his brother's promise to hand over the Pikachu plushie and be nice for three days straight. Watching the whole thing go down, I wonder if this is a good deal or if he could have gotten more, too tired to intervene in the LEGO Land politics anymore I resign myself, at times, to crying and listening to "Extraordinary Machine" while they destroy everything, jumping on the top bunk and slamming heads into dressers and painting the walls green, dragging the dogs by their legs and slamming GoGurts by the box, refashioning them afterward into robot costumes and throwing the sticky plastic on the carpet, linoleum and hardwood, the trauma of cleaning these three very different surfaces reinvigorating my drive toward the vasectomy imagining a control over my personal space that will never again exist. In the chaos I often manage to pay 7/13 overdue bills and consider, but never quite finish the thought of a fine sentence or line of poetry, saving the resolve for later and later and, pausing, BumblebeeFort might stop and ask, "Daddy, why do bears exist?" And his brother apologizes. "Sorry," he says, "I won't say that I will fucking kill you anymore."

And GodRex96, well, is old now and through a combination of the world beating the sensitivity out of him, the horror of hormones, and generalized human selfishness gives zero fucks about anything other than what he wants and can easily attain, through violence or otherwise; I miss the old him, and lament the loss of a future person in myself who could be a better father to any of them.

"Kids is fine," I say to my great-grandmother. "Kids is fine."

"That's good, that's good Joey," she says, talking faster and stuttering more than either of her sons for whom it has taken me my whole life to understand. "You know my lil knuckleheads can't even take care of themselves out here can't even take care a theyself."

It would be hard to comment on her oldest son, the man who in lieu of a mother or father sort of raised me, raised all of us. He's dying a few rooms down and has been doing so for quite some time, unable to speak and so imagined, unable to feel. I'd been bitter and pretentious about the things he'd done, the beatings and the cursing, mostly of me and my grandmother, and much less attentive to what he'd made possible my whole life.

This was easier, the former, as I'd entered a life genre where men like him were more easily dismissed. For a decade I refused to speak to him or help him survive while on the other hand, spending all I had in time and energy and emotion on my mother, whom I barely knew, who barely knew me. There was something about this not knowing that made her more viable as a human being; it meant that I could see her hurt, and in need of less hurt, and myself as her son, capable of some form of alleviation. My grandfather on the other hand was a done deal, a broken man who represented each and everything wrong with us, despite being the person who, more than anyone else, made me possible. In liberal parlance, he was a monster. Only now after having failed so miserably and for so long to rehabilitate, or to make my mother happy, did I even contemplate speaking to this man, giving him the time of day after he'd given us his life, but it was too late. And maybe too easy to use my bio dad as a substitute. Ray would say also, not worth the time; Lise always thought he was funny. It is true though that he could stimulate laughter, mostly in women, as was our shared necessity.

Complaining to my great-grandmother, which is hard to distinguish from just telling the truth, feels out of the question. I don't describe how every second of every day I feel like I'm failing them and they're disappointing me, how I'm afraid that the development of their awareness of the world and attention to details is too slow and I am too tired to go any further, and that I might die long before they are able to care for themselves in even the most basic matters, let alone be helpful, rather than harmful, to anyone else; I say everything is fine, and they're fine. We talk for a bit about her dead and dying sons as I empty her urine into a cup. SGT Williams, who stood up for us heavy with all the racist reiterations in the army, is in the next room. "Doc," he says, "what up man!" and I dap him up and refill his water, promising to update him on his discharge status soon; his roommate is one of the old Jewish women from the Main Line who can't stand niggers and throws things anytime a black person comes in to help her, so Lise and them trot off with a *just let the bitch die* attitude till Melissa or somebody comes to check on her; in the room after that, same as over twelve hours ago, is Ms. Johnson, awake now and soiled again. When I walk in Lise is already in there with the new recruit, a young Indian girl who looks at me like I'm an anomaly. I'm in denial about feeling ill, a nausea that won't go away no matter what I swallow from the med drawer.

"Girl," Lise says. "Do not look at that boy like that he done been ran through."

The new girl looks shocked at her introduction to the hospital.

"Oh my god!" Ms. Johnson says, laughing. "Don't talk about my friend like that!"

"You better getcha friend then Ms. Johnson."

"This is an unsafe work environment," I say, tossing the dirty linen from the floor into the bin, mostly just urine. "How you feel, Ms. Johnson?"

She side-eyes me a bit. "Well, I'm in the dang hospital again, so—"

"Okay, okay," I say. "You know what I mean."

"Yall got any of them muffins?" she says.

—

NOT A HALF HOUR after being up on Med Surg I see the two guards come rolling up behind D, who's pushing Rell on the stretcher. They put him just a few rooms away from my great-grandmother, and for whatever reason I remember that I still hadn't given this man the apple juice. I'll bring it in later, since now, even from afar at the computer, I can tell he's sound asleep. With the call bells answered and the new admission already knocked out I can try to gather myself and reassess the host of potential problems at home and at work. The sixth floor's problems are that they are neither urgent nor terminal, thus making them the most difficult, and arguably most important, to articulate: You are not dying, but you are. You do not need to stay in the hospital, but maybe you do. You must imbue actions, by force, with equal importance: charting the Activities of Daily Living and draining catheters, the occasional code or respiratory distress that you might not notice at first while charting ADLs and draining catheters. You're doing more, minute to minute than in the ED, but your mind has more space to roam. Rotation displaces anticipation. But you often forget your location, imbuing the daily with modes of urgency. You see the necessity of call bells being answered now, piss evacuated, shit scrubbed up, conversational comforts amused immediately; your colleagues think you're crazy; your body thinks you're crazy.

My body reminds me of a certain exhaustion by adding an ache in my left leg to the nausea. I think about all the young bouls in the morgue and my retreat into work, think about the bills and Belize, think about Tierra and death as I text her to cancel the fantasy, think about how much better things were in the desert. Think about how Ray and I played *Borderlands* in Baghdad, this Mad Max loot-grabbing slaughter of an RPG, tearing heads and dropping cel-shaded cartoon bodies like we ain't have real jobs at all. Like we were never tired. The avatars wore hockey masks and brandished golden guns, threw portal grenades and shape-shifted and fell dead often, melting into squishy clumps of goo, but they always got back up. We considered suicide together, Ray and I, Skyped lovers in Philly when the other was away from their twin-sized bed, and we took a lot of Benadryl but could never sleep even if there was time. We watched *The Office* with subtitles under the blaring of the phalanx gun and decided, Ray and

I together, without words, that we'd one hundred per-cent *Borderlands* and commenced the marathon of our lifetimes splashing, shooting, ducking and covering through its utopic dystopia like our lives depended on it. In daylight we ate at Popeyes and Cinnabon, oblit-erating smoothies and dark meat three-pieces, we car-ried heavy metal to and from the PX grabbing snacks and tools and games, got fitted for cheap suits down the road and ran laps at the gym, slept a few hours beside each other and imagined we were kin. At home and out-side the gates people died, constantly; we were directly and indirectly the cause and could quit but didn't, because we either didn't have to look at them dying or had already looked too much. Ray hated the fetishiza-tion of resistance, refusal. We took shirtless pictures in our boots and fatigues and shared them back home; Lise claimed to have masturbated to them; every other man, woman or gender-nonconforming person without home training wanted to fuck Ray and explained to me in vivid detail what they would do to his body, his body that I can finally admit will never move again. And this consideration winds me down with its unreality, makes me weightless but unable to move. All I can do is think, to remember.

A goofy white boy in our platoon shot at me, point-blank, "by accident"; our platoon sergeant lifted him from the ground like a child and slammed him into our truck, screaming like any good father would, before Ray stomped him out. At night we searched for bombs along long dirt roads where diplomats might travel, powerful people whose lives were infinitely more important to the continued circulation of capital, who talked clean and bombed hospitals and whose decorum, when we were in their presence, mandated that we not curse or fart or indicate any potential for sensation; it was great preparation for college. We licked windows and scoured sand for suspicious activity, but the best thing about deployment was not having to pay rent, desperate as most of us were to secure housing for ourselves and our families back home; we would have done anything, let the army do anything to our bodies; it was but one reason why men barely in their thirties had been overseas three or four times already, having come back to noise and little else in their homes, absent the love of flag or country. This was disappointing for a junior ethnographer such as myself, a Northerner who'd heard the stories about army boys riding and dying for the country hardcore. Most white boys in Iraq, who wore the same uniform we did, became too much like us; they wanted the whole affair over with and despite this we all had some urge to go back. But any of us would easily have killed another boy; it didn't have to be anyone specific nor for any lofty project; the simple fact was that we were boys who grew up in America, and in one way or another, this was just our primary mode of communication.

I was tryna remember what genre or tense I shoulda been in, but mostly, we were bored.

Each night we'd drive around all night at fifteen miles an hour in MRAPs—Mine-Resistant Ambush-Protected, or "big on the outside, small on the inside" vehicles—looking for bombs. Your back hurts the whole time and it's either too hot or too cold, always cramped. We ate the Otises. Fitting then that we'd signed up, that is, filled out the Army National Guard's job application, at the same time as those for Lowe's and KFC, City Blue and Delta Airlines, Old Navy and nursing homes in West Philly.

Finding a bomb typically meant one blew up on someone's truck or person, which was the plan, of course. "Found" was synonymous with "blown up." The linguistic trickery here was low-level like the word "freedom," which sublimated most of the fear and anxiety that rational people, were any of us rational, should have had in such situations. Most of the time no one got hurt, though in other instances, vehicles were destroyed. Crumpled. Doors were blown off, windows were breached. We'd have to switch out all our gear from the busted vehicle to a new one: mic sets, stretchers, long spine boards, walk kits, seat cushions, backpacks, snacks, 240 rounds of 5.56 each, the 240B from the gunner's hatch, and most importantly, one if not several coolers packed to the brim with ice, Reese's Cups, Twizzlers, bananas, Krimpets, Red Bull and Rip

Its and Otis Spunkmeyer muffins, preferably chocolate. Straining your back while moving a cooler was a rite of passage; being hurt was proof of the proper use of the body.

The last time an IED went off, it hit the third vehicle in our convoy of six. It was late but we were on a wide city street with lights on both sides that looked like 676, not the more infamous route Vernon, but some other one whose name I can't remember. The rubble was still crackling down to the road and dinging off the hoods of our trucks when the LT got on the radio:

THREE Ds? BREAK. WHAT'S YOUR STATUS? OVER.

FUCK, said Shick, the driver, over the radio, keying his mic in anger. I'M NOT MOVING THIS FUCKING COOLER AGAIN.

The vehicle was deadlined. And the contents of those coolers were not to be played with. Since we were often on missions for twelve or more hours, and overnight too, we would miss chow a lot—sometimes dinner, other times breakfast. Forgetting to pack the cooler could—for those prone to dramatization, I'd say ninety percent—be the start of a four-act play littered with the empty platitudes of male insecurity and every petty, otherwise ignorable slight that occurred since we got in-country. I'm not sure when I first heard the word "hangry," but I know that the army is where it mattered. The actual mission prep—the briefing, checking equipment, sensitive items, making sure the radios and crew systems were up and all that—was secondary to junk food stocking. Some soldiers would carry their own body weight in tuna, beef jerky, elk jerky, deer jerky, Twizzlers, Scooby Doo snacks, Rice Krispies, Doritos, Red Bull, etc. The muffins though were the only good thing we got for free besides tinnitus. There were also cans of baby-sized Rip It energy drinks that only seemed to come in grape, though Ray and I would take notice of other soldiers with red or blue ones. Since we both worked in the same truck, the last one—me as medic, and Ray as my Combat Life Saver (CLS)—we had the snack game down to a science. Whenever supply got a new shipment of Otises or Rip Its in, I'd be right there by the little rickety shack to claim at least one whole box. It was important to have variety on the muffins, so I don't hesitate to admit now that I would use my power as a medic—I need to have food and water in my truck first in case of emergencies—to rat-fuck the banana and blueberry packages of Otis and replace half the chocolate with a mix of those lesser flavors. Then I would guard them until Ray came over to transport our personal box, along with some Rip Its, to the big blue cooler. By that time the rest of the platoon would realize the supply door was open and storm the gates, leaving nothing but crumbs and torn plastic out front, swirling into baby tornadoes of sand.

It would not be unreasonable to think that Ray and I's entire relationship was born atop the cellophane corpses of Otis Spunkmeyer. Sure, we might have become friends eventually, but never like Lady and the Tramp over crinkled wrappers, our feet propped up on the cooler, debating the greatest bars of André 3000 and Nas, reminiscing about our finest *Call of Duty* kill cam moments and the white tears that followed from Baker, Nelson and Miller (Scrappy was of course on our team). It was there, in the back of a little MRAP one prior night, that we'd even conceived a way to change the whole game of our Iraq deployment. Where we decided to link the entire platoon together. Even our platoon sergeant had asked to get in on the game before, but couldn't with the garbage Wi-Fi on base that, naturally, we all paid $80.00 a month for. With enough Cat 5 cable and a little sweat Ray and I amassed a network rivaling at least T-Mobile's, forever changing our fates and improving the overall discourse en route, since we could bask for hours in the relatively neutral arena of shit-talking on the game, until Scrappy, from the lead vehicle, came over the radio.

ALL STOP! he said.

Ray chucked the chocolate muffin I'd asked for hours ago at my face. Normally I'd have tried to catch it in my mouth like at Hibachi, but I always got still when there was an "all stop," stressed about the potential implication that I would have to act. The lone medic responsible for an entire platoon, a nineteen-year-old who, previously, could hardly muster the courage to play basketball in front of new people, was now directly responsible for thirty lives. It meant that I was always running scenarios in my head, mechanisms of injury and possible fallouts, if X, then Y, how to treat burns and eviscerations, check for TBIs, sucking chest wounds and crush injuries, lost limbs and open fractures. I had practiced beyond redundancy, bloated my brain with potential responses to trauma, its synapses racing toward solutions, always. Always thinking, all night every night, of what might happen and how bad, of how repair was my responsibility and mine alone. Back home I'd wake each night sweating, imagining my child crying and at risk of death only to find The Old One, not yet GodRex96, sound asleep folded into the corner of his bed.

Our vehicle comes to a sharp halt. The muffin bounces lightly, but dense along the floor. Ray puts his feet right back up on the cooler, bobbing his head to his music. He's worried too, about what might happen, though he has complete faith in me; if anybody really gets hurt, he'll simply follow my lead.

Every other vehicle freezes. Normally we're traveling so slow you can barely perceive the movement, but the jolt of a sudden stop wakes up most of the rear seaters. Window lickers rise in unison. Rogers, up in the gunner's hatch, rocks back and forth, knocking his helmet against the opening. Those dudes feel every-thing. We all look around, doing our 5s and 25s.

Scrappy comes in over the radio again.

LOOKS LIKE WE GOT A COPPER WIRE.

BREAK.

ABOUT FIFTEEN METERS AHEAD AT MY TEN O'CLOCK.

BREAK.

IT LEADS SOMEWHERE OFF THE ROAD.

LT Kutanis: ROGER THAT, GO AHEAD AND INTERROGATE.

Scrappy rides up front in the Husky, a single-man vehicle with a mine-interrogating claw that looks like it grew up on a cartoon farm, like him. Ray finds it cruel to be in the lead vehicle alone, but agrees with the sound economic decision, considering that the platoon would only lose one person when Scrappy gets blown up. But when Scrappy takes too long to respond, it makes Ray uncomfortable in ways he would never let show.

ROGER THAT.

In the last vehicle we can hardly see anything. At most, if we squeeze up into the front compartment with the platoon sergeant and driver, we might catch a flash, see the smoke and sand and dirt and trash billowing up into a volcanic cloud of refuse. We might be able to stare as the cloud, after an explosion, dissipates over time, los-ing isotopes of trash bags and grains of sand. We could typically hear the thump of a bomb up ahead, but the trickling down of rocks from the sky that goes on for minutes afterward is always more pronounced, but, tired as we are, it is more likely we hallucinate than identify a threat before a threat identifies the threat in us. So we stay bunched up at the front of the vehicle, hoping to catch a flash.

While the arm of the Husky fiddles with wires, Robinson, our driver, turns to look at us: Me, Ray, SGT Mason, and our LT in the passenger seat.

"So how many toddlers do you think you could take in a fight?" he says.

"I dunno, like thirty," says Ray. Much quicker than I can comprehend, he has a clear image of himself dispatching droves of greasy toddlers by the truckload in some schoolyard. "Prolly hand-to-hand at first, then with a shovel or whatever object I can find lying around. From an aerial view it would look like *Dynasty Warriors*."

"Wait, what?" I say.

"Thirty seem like a lot?" He considers bumping the number up; perhaps he underestimated himself.

"Yall are weak as shit, I'd kill like forty-five minimum," says SGT Mason.

"As a medical professional," I say, "I'd just like to point out that our platoon sergeant was the first to mention *killing* the toddlers."

"Well what's the point of fightin em"—SGT Mason removes his helmet and rearranges his body armor to squeeze around in his seat and face us—"if you're not gonna kill em? Seems like a waste of time and energy, what, lock em up as punishment or kill them later? These kinds of considerations are exactly why I'm in charge."

"He's got a point," Ray says, chewing a muffin. "And I think I wanna change my answer to like, seventy-five."

"Yeah I guess, if like all the toddlers were vampires or something, there'd be reason to slaughter them," I say.

"Okay Twilight," says Robinson. "I was just curious about the toddler thing and Doc somehow brings it back to the vampires."

It is true, Ray considers in passin, that I very often bring conversations back around to the vampires. Somebody keys their mic before Ray can speak again.

*Heavy breathing over the radio.*

LT Kutanis: SCRAP COME IN.

Scrappy: WIRE DOESN'T LEAD ANYWHERE. BREAK.

CLEAR TO CHARLIE MIKE.

LT Kutanis: ROGER THAT.

"Why the fuck was this asshole breathing all heavy on the radio then? Scared the shit outta me," says SGT Mason. Then he turns forward, eyes to the road.

Romero shifts to the back of the vehicle again and I follow as the truck starts moving. We stare at each other for a second, then Ray keys up his mic and breathes heavily on the radio. Extra, like a rhino asleep in a cave.

LT Kutanis: DO NOT PLAY ON THE PLA-TOON NET.

We laugh, as does SGT Mason up front.

SGT Mason keys up his mic and breathes heavily on the radio.

And so it goes for hours on the road until we all fall silent, drifting into the potential of lives elsewhere.


Scrappy: YOU KNOW THEY USED TO HAVE DUDES OUT HERE LIKE ACTUALLY SHOVELING SHIT INTO A PILE AND BURNING IT??!

BREAK.

AND THEY WERE JUST STANDING NEXT TO IT LIKE A BUNCH OF DUMB ASSES.

THEY WOULD GET SICK AND NEVER THINK IT WAS THE AIR.

BREAK.

MOTHERFUCKERS ARE SO FUCKIN STU-PID MAN.

He's clearly talking to Ray and I, maybe Baby Snoop and Brown too, but since he's in the first truck, alone, he has to key up his mic and speak to the whole platoon at once, an indication of his loneliness and fatigue. It was silent again for a little while.

"Is this nigga really talkin about this on the platoon

net?" Ray asks me, squinching up his face and handing me another muffin.

"I mean, that's what it sound like," I say.

"Whatever, fuck it."

Ray: YOU KNOW YOU WOULDA BEEN RIGHT THERE SHOVELIN AND BURNIN SCRAP!

Rogers laughs but doesn't key up his mic to say anything.

FUCK OUTTA HERE, I WOULDA DECLINED THAT SHIT.

BREAK.

PUN INTENDED.

BREAK.

THEY WOULDA HAD ME ALL THE WAY FUCKED UP OUT HERE—

ALRIGHT. SHUT THE FUCK UP WITH THE NONSENSE OVER PLATOON NET.

LT Kutanis: OKAY YOU BUTT BUDDIES CAN PLAY WITH EACH OTHER WHEN WE ARE FINISHED. STAY THE FUCK OFF THE NET.

Ray: OOOOOHH YOU HOES DONE GOT LT MAD.

Ray and I laugh across from each other, our legs propped up on opposite benches now. In the lull we discuss love. How to satisfy his girl back home, to make up for our fathers', and fathers' fathers' and fathers' fathers' fathers', crimes of heart and hearth. We reminisce on the loss of innocence never ours to be lost and the quiet shame of having been born ourselves and to our fathers, and in our neighborhoods. Ray is configuring the grand gesture to end all grand gestures disguised as consistent love for his lover. She does not want a ring or a necklace or a house full of things but consistency, that thing that is harder to come by. He signs a lease with her and her cats, squeals *I love you*s in and out of context and hails the overwhelming power not of her pussy but her mind. He is doing this right, assured by himself, and in my silence it feels so wrong. What would it take, he wants to know, to maintain this feeling? And how could he make a different decision than to tell me, years later when I asked how they'd split, that he simply couldn't afford to be in a relationship, despite how also true this was.

Gravel pops against the underside of our truck, tires crunching through the desert-city-desert past T-wall after T-wall after sometimes broken T-wall all through the night. We could no longer have electronics. Some dickhead had pulled out his PSP in the middle of a mission and started playing it on full volume while the battalion commander was on a ride-along, sitting right next to him. After that we had to toss the iPods and Game Boys and even our interpreter who otherwise watched hardcore porn lying supine on the stretcher for hours every night had to join us in the sour pageantry of uniformed staring at each other, in silence. The LT never said who fucked up, probably for the fear that the perpetrator might be killed.

ALL STOP!

There are some dings. Little ticks in rapid succession, even though our vehicle isn't moving anymore.

"What the hell is that?" I say to Ray.

He just shrugs and opens a pack of Scooby Doo snacks.

CHARLIE MIKE!

GUNNERS KEEP YOUR HEADS ON A SWIVEL. SMALL ARMS FIRE.

BREAK.

EIGHT O'CLOCK.

LT: IF YOU SEE SOMETHING, CALL IT OUT.

ROGER THAT.

READ YOU LIMA CHARLIE SIR.

We keep rolling.

Most of the guys in our platoon don't trust Scrap in the first vehicle, though not a single one of them would volunteer to take his place. They say, *That vehicle was designed to dig up bombs, but Scrap was designed to cook crystal meth.* He looks the part, but whatever his true roots, he has more in common with us than with them. Scrap could talk shit almost like he went to public high school in the city and refused the more subtle alliances of his lacking pigment just enough for Ray to tolerate him. The first time me and Romero heard him call SPC Wright an "Ol weak ass let ya girl make you player two ass dude" while playing *Duty*, the lines were drawn.

Scrap couldn't play ball for shit though, and he knew it. Still, at least he could pass. And every time Ray almost got into a scuffle, Scrap never snitched. What Scrap couldn't do well, though, was shut the fuck up. Ever. It was insane to imagine him not talking to himself or doing anything else during those twelve-hour missions. He had to be climbing up the walls in that little box of a vehicle; he wasn't even five feet tall and could barely fit. What else could he do but divert all that hog-tied energy into looking for bombs?

Scrap called out everything that wasn't an IED, and then some. Not fifteen minutes after the small arms fire, he's on the radio again.

ALL STOP!

We trickle to a halt, keeping fifty meters apart. Robinson puts the brake on and lets out an exaggerated sigh. "What the fuck does he think he found this time? Prolly like a trash bag, or two trash bags or some dumb shit. God, he's always wasting our fucking time. I'm tryna get back in time for chow."

"You always bitchin," Ray says. "You'd be bitchin if they said we could go home tomorrow, wit ya bitch ass."

SGT Mason laughs. "I bet he's gonna say it's a copper wire. And you are always bitching, Robinson."

My mouth is full of Otis, that chocolaty goodness.

I'm about to finish chewing and speak when Scrap comes in over the radio.

LOOKS LIKE A COPPER WIRE, UNDER SOME TRASH.

BREAK.

I'M GONNA INTERROGATE. OVER.

LT: GO AHEAD SCRAPPY...

"Called it," SGT Mason says.

Minutes pass quietly. I start sweating, hoping it isn't a bomb and I'll have to pick up little pieces of Scrap off the highway. I run through a few scenarios: What if an arm gets blown off? Easy, throw on a high-and-tight tourniquet, then throw his ass in the back of the ambulance, hit the HABCs. What if his face was burnt, his airway closing? Not a problem, I had a cric kit in my bag and three inside the RG-33 and that was always my quickest skill in medic school. What if he was already dead when I got there? Fuck. Would I even know what to do? What if I just froze up and stared into space?

The anxiety was so bad so often that I'd hope to be the injured party myself, so that I wouldn't have the burden, the fear of fucking it up for someone else, of almost but then not saving someone's life, of the permanent failure. Sure, most people who got blown up were either going to live or die no matter what I do, but everyone doesn't know that, nor would they care. It would all be on me, and I could never figure out if I was ready for that kind of responsibility, or if I ever would be.

The tense few minutes of mouth breathing on the mics go by as they do during every possible IED interrogation.

"You have got to be fucking kidding me!" yelled Robinson on the internals, just our truck. "Did yall see that?"

I jump at first, but there isn't any explosion. Then, I'm relieved by the quiet.

"You know we can't see back here," Romero says.

"I know I didn't just see what I thought I saw," says Robinson.

"What?" SGT Mason says.

Scrap comes in over the radio.

ALL CLEAR.

Our LT laughs all over the platoon net.

ROGER THAT SCRAPPY. CHARLIE MIKE.

Robinson keys up his mic.

SCRAP DID YOU JUST STOP US FOR A FUCK-ING PIGEON?

WHEN WE RETURN IN the morning, the chow hall is already closed. Each driver parks their vehicles slowly, in a fit of toddler-like hangry pains, as if there was no longer a reason to be finished for the night. Why bother leaving the cool AC of the vehicles? The sun was up, and it'd be a hundred degrees again soon; and the motor pool was especially susceptible to the heat, crowded with all the clunky hunks of metal and ankle-breaking rocks that made soldiers high-step, extra carefully, doubling energy expenditures and globs of warm sweat underneath the hundred pounds of gear they carried to and from their vehicles every day. As everyone grabs their bags to dismount, Scrappy jogs to catch up with me and Ray as we walk toward our CHU.

"Yo, LT was mad as shit," he says, laughing.

Ray laughs too. "He always mad. I woulda kept goin though, fuck em."

I reshoulder my aid bag, exhausted.

"You want help carrying that stuff Doc?" says Scrappy.

"Nah I got it man," I say. "Thank you though."

Two other soldiers, Smith and Froman, walk by us, bumping hard into Scrappy.

"Dumb ass," Smith mumbles in passing. Froman says something under his breath about wasting time and making them miss breakfast, but the word "dickhead" is the clearest.

"Fuck you say, pussy?" Scrappy drops his assault pack on the rocks.

"What?" Smith says, turning around and stepping out his stride toward Scrappy.

Zero to a hundred. It's what we're trained for, where training counts. The last time this happened it was Ray who flipped the switch. He was in the shower a few stalls away from me, but Smith and Froman, that whole upstate PA crew, and a few Wisconsin guys were already in the shower stalls across from him. I was singing to myself like nobody was around, but Ray was quiet, listening in on the chatter. With the curtains closed we couldn't see each other, but voices were easy to distinguish, and Taylor had left his Superman towel hanging in plain view.

"There's a lot of them ain't it?" Taylor, one of the Wisconsin guys, said. "And are they all like that?" he went on. "I mean you're cool Smith, but..."

"I dunno man, that's those motherfuckers from Philly. Nothing but ghetto trash out there," Smith said.

They laughed in unison.

"We all started calling them crackheads and convicts," Taylor said, "Instead of tryna tell em apart."

They all laughed again, louder.

"And yall got one as yall's medic too. I wouldn't trust that shit," said Taylor. "Prolly get you all killed."

Ray could have kept his presence and frustration unknown. He could have stuck behind the thin cover of shower curtain, regardless of how little it did to brunt the force of such regular contempt. He'd done so plenty of times before. There wasn't enough energy in all of Iraq to go off on a flock of white boys for every slight, every time; hell, not two days ago he'd let this guy's bodega comments slide during mission prep. He also knew that leadership took complaints about "that race bullshit" about as seriously as sexual assault; the SHARP classes I used to teach having by then become little more than inspiration for jokes. The last time race came up, politely, it turned into the commander announcing to our whole platoon—while staring at me, Ray, Washington and Brown—that he didn't care "if your baby mommas are in the twelfth circle of hell surrounded by raging pit bulls," we all need to be focusing on the mission, "end of story."

And Ray let that slide too.

But then, in the showers, hearing them question my ability, made Ray forget that he was not to make waves, so he hopped out of the shower in a hurry, not bothering to dry off, just pulling his PT clothes and sandals on wet, and stepped out into the dark. When Smith and Taylor came out, he grabbed Taylor by the throat and slammed his head against the concrete outside the bathrooms. The sound of skull hitting rock like that was almost as terrifying as the fact that Ray didn't stop. He slammed Taylor's head over and over, though his eyes went white after the first strike. Ray dropped Smith too like it was nothing, treated him like a toy and went back to crushing Taylor's skull. The scuffle was more sad than anything, and I pretended I was tryna break it up when folks came over, grabbing Ray and escorting him off the scene saying they weren't even worth it.

"It's your life," I said over and over. "You gotta be worth something, not them."

Though now, was he willing to do the same for Scrap? Smith came range-walking across the gravel toward Scrappy with that look on his face, the one that skips schoolyard shoving and goes straight to knuckles, though he hadn't dropped his rifle yet. Scrappy tossed his M4 down and raised his hands before Smith came within arm's reach. It was cute almost, all five feet of him in a rare state of seriousness, intent on dismantling a man who could curl Scrap's whole body, gear on and all. But Smith stopped before anything could happen. Before Ray could intervene, before I might play peacemaker. The LT stood a few feet behind Scrap.

"What are you all doing here still?" he said.

We all turned to him, acting unsurprised.

"Just musculoskeletal stuff, sir," I said. "Scrappy is having problems with his back. I told him to drop his gear so I could look at him."

Smith and Froman had walked away. The LT saw them going but didn't bother questioning them. Ray went along with me, securing Scrap's weapon and gear.

The LT was only half buying it but was too tired to bother. "Out here, in the heat?" he asked. "How about you all go back to your rooms and sleep, or if he's that bad, take him to the TMC."

"Roger that sir," we all said, also known as *Go fuck yourself sir* and a bunch of other things one might not say directly to leadership.

Scrappy will get blown up plenty of times fine, then overdose during demobilization. He'll have a girl he meets on Tinder bring him heroin and I'll find him ass naked half under the covers, half out, her shivering and crying in a corner, trying to explain to me what happened and I'll ask her to leave rather than implicate her in it. His body will already be too cold for the hospital, though warm enough and close enough to feel like we failed him.

I'D ALMOST FORGOTTEN THE apple juice entirely when I notice the call bell ringing. Many call bells at once, waking me from what I knew would happen the instant I sat down, my mouth tasting stale after falling asleep without brushing. But just then as I get up to grab the juice and deliver my bio dad from thirst I hear someone scream beyond the nurses' station. In a flash Rell passes by the charge desk, cuff still hangin from his hand and, when one of the nurses tries to stop him, he batters her with a rolling chair and keeps moving, past Lise who jumps outta the way as he sprints straight to the emergency exit stairs, blood and maggots trailing in his footprints. The other guard who was supposed to be with him comes outta the bathroom and speed-walks to his partner as me and Melissa pick up our nurse from the floor and settle her on a stretcher. From the back room where Rell was the other guard screams, and when

Lise and I enter to the blood, the TV is still playing Toonami and the guard is on the floor with his face ravaged, one hand clinging to his gun as he seizes. Lise and I, looking at each other, both consider the alternative outcomes here, the what-ifs had Rell successfully taken the gun. We have to pick the guard up and take him down to trauma too. Security is all over, searching for Rell, and downstairs in the ED. Everybody's panicking and furious, yelling, *How the fuck could this happen?* And *Where was the guards?!*

The nurses not actively working in the bay are ducked down behind their desks or guarding patient rooms, scrambling to lock doors and looking over their shoulders; it takes a while before I realize, given the looks, that I'm expected to look for Rell too, though what I'm expected to do once he's found is less clear than it's ever been. I walk just quick enough to suggest urgency, but slow enough that the other men pass me, scanning the exits, past the main ED doors and stock room, through the X-ray and CT areas where the terror is most complete and frozen, nurses ducking under desks and patients waiting for tests bewildered, and through triage and downstairs, toward the revolving doors that exit out to the Halal truck by the bus station and right there, unmistakable, I see him halfway between freedom and everything else. It's Rell, pummeling the registration lady who usually walks in and out of those doors on smoke breaks and who has on occasion, barred the path of other AWOL patients. He doesn't even notice me in his pleasure, as I've been taught to imagine him. A security guard, not intervening but rather blocking his path of flight beyond the revolving door, is planning to react, though not reactive enough. A doctor yells and jumps on top of Rell, catching an elbow before Rell turns around to pummel him too, and it's hard not to hear people in the background begging him to stop; Rell climbs on top of this doctor and beats him bloody into the linoleum as I stand there, too precious for action and waiting for more security guards to come and detain him. Or, perusing the available options, I decide otherwise. Desperate, I grab him from behind, sliding his chin above the crook of my elbow, where parents tell wayward children they should cough or sneeze. I do this gently, and with maximum force. I'm holding him. And when I squeeze, he feels warm, his back tight against my chest, his braids up in my nose, smelling the way they do.

Is he struggling?

When I whisper to him, he doesn't respond, at least not clearly enough for me to answer, but there's so much I want to ask him. Descriptions of his life and my mother, where he comes from, and where he might have seen his life going. What about the kids, my other siblings? How are they doing? He's kicking now, in the air and at the floor, making things difficult. To the question of how he feels, I sense confusion but he only mumbles something, slowing down, which overwhelms me with the urge to squeeze tighter, to force him alive again. Ignoring the pop in my arm I can feel tears climbing down past his mouth and then slowly, the acquiescence, the relief that it's finally over. And despite this we're stuck; I can't stop squeezing him. This I realize only because they put us both on a stretcher together, for which I'm thankful. So thankful for the colleagues surrounding us now, asking me if I'm okay or if I might please let go? Thankful for that bit of Johnny's nasty goulash, the Twizzlers from Louie's pocket, the chocolate behind the charge desk, and every Otis Ray and I stashed in the back of that truck, so thankful for the surrounding concern, the trepidation in their eyes as they ask if I can hear them or not, the light flashing past my eyelids and all the gloved hands attending to my needs, so thankful not to be alone, to be here, in community, to feel held in my narrowing field of perception as I lean, with too much left undone, into something resembling rest.

# *Acknowledgments*

Thank you Aisha for telling me when I'm being ridiculous just as much as when I'm not. Thank you to Cathy, Isle, and Elias in the Murder of Crows, for tolerating the prose. Thank you to my mom and them for being real even when it doesn't pay, and trying, always trying to be better than the models before us. Thank you lovers and friends, especially Clarence and Wais and Drake, for hanging in there all these years. Thank you to Simone for being "intimate and unsentimental with everyone" as an ongoing lesson in politics, social relations, and even parenthood. Thank you PJ and Maddie and Roxanne for taking this work and risk seriously even when it's difficult. Thank you to them people who live in my house, love yall. And thank you to everybody I ever worked with from Sterling Glen and the army and Atlanta Bread Company all the way to EMS and Home Depot and everything in-between.

# *About the Author*

**JOSEPH EARL THOMAS** IS a writer from Frankford whose work has appeared or is forthcoming in *VQR, N+1, Gulf Coast,* the *Offing,* and the *Kenyon Review.* He has an MFA in prose from the University of Notre Dame and is a doctoral candidate in English at the University of Pennsylvania. An excerpt of his memoir, *Sink,* won the 2020 Chautauqua Janus Prize, and he has received fellowships from Fulbright, VONA, Tin House, and Bread Loaf. He's writing a collection of stories, *Leviathan Beach,* among other oddities.